A TRILOGY

DICMATIZED: THE DOCTOR IS IN

SEXCAPADES : VOLUME I
WRITTEN BY: DYPHIA aka Gemini Phoenix

 ISBN-13: 978-0615652696

 Edited by: Dyphia

Consulting Editors: Tiara Brown, Tracie Holmes

Cover Created by: Dyphia

Cover Model: Nicky Richardson

Written by: Dyphia

Contact Info: visit www.dyphiablount.com

Email: msgeminiphoenix@gmail.com

Follow Dyphia at www.sexualhealingspot.com

DEDICATIONS

I would like to thank God for blessing me with the talent to overcome obstacles, and the dedication to finish.

I have to say a special Thank you to Neiima Edwards for inspiring me to write this book from my Blackberry. I want to thank my loving husband, Shelton, who helped me keep the mood and pace of this love story.

I want to thank Sandra B., Jasmine W., and Yonsmine T. as well as my other family and friends for keeping me inspired to finish the story.

Last, but certainly not least, I want to thank my three beautiful children: La'Cheyla, LaNea, and Dominique who look up to me and respect me no matter what I choose to do with my life.

Chapter 1

I'm A Beast

As Dr. Lenese Stringfield leans back in her chair with her feet propped up and crossed on her desk, she thinks, *Finally some peace and quiet.* It is a quarter to seven and the last clients for the day are just leaving. Lenese feels beat. Between her sex thirsty clients and the recurring nightmare, her days are getting longer which is really getting the best of her now. *Sleep? What is that?* She closes her eyes and prays for a little relaxation before the long drive home. Suddenly her legs fall open and she wonders, *Is there enough time?*

Reclining back in the beautifully hand crafted, mahogany, swivel desk chair given to her by one of her favorite clients, Lamont Massenburg, and smiles, *There is always time.* She takes a trip down memory lane and pictures Lamont crying out for mercy, watching his work of art shrivel up to nothing as she pulls every ounce of being and life out of it with her lips alone. *Damn, I'm good!*

She gradually slides her hand down her pants and between the dampness of her thighs sticking together from the moisture. Using her pinky finger to move her black lace thong to the side, she brushes across her pussy piercing with ease and immediately starts to cum.

Smirking and puckering up her lick able, luxurious lips, she snaps out of the trance and pulls out her gloss to smooth them over. *You're a beast with these things.*

He is only one of many that will always appreciate the magnitude of services she offers to ensure her practice remains in the top three percentile in Atlanta. Lenese will do almost anything to make sure her business stays on top with no shame in her game. In fact, it is a very exciting feeling when her work is complete and all her clients leave happy and very satisfied.

All men want her, and all women respect her. Growing up in the projects made her realize that she has to use what has to get what she wants; a lesson learned at a very early age. From seeing her friends hooked on crack and being gunned down in the streets, to being raped and molested by people she thought she could trust; Lenese had been through a lot which forced her to take her life in her own hands, and without dictation.

Dr. Stringfield has been the best sex therapist for the last five years of her practice. No one knows how her ranking in marriage counseling is so high, and never will. She teaches the men how to be the perfect sex partners and make the women forget all the other issues. They become "Dicmatized" so to speak.

People seem to get so caught up in financial issues and other problems, that they usually let their sex lives slide down-hill in the meantime. While teaching them to understand how a healthy sexual relationship can make all other problems fade away, her techniques bring couples back to the feelings they had when they first started dating.

Lenese doesn't remember herself being fine back in the day. In fact, she felt quite plain back then. All of her cousins are guys so, caring to be a 'girly girl' was never a top priority. However, she learned the game from them--how men and women both think and react to certain things.

Lenese hated her lips growing up and remembers her junior high school boyfriend, Jason, telling her that she was cute from the nose up. That made her really self- conscience about her looks and a little ashamed. Now, men can't get enough of fantasizing about her luxurious lips and aggressive sexual behavior that is soon to follow.

Lenese is a Gemini; the sign of twins, and often considers herself to be 'the forbidden fruit.' No ONE man can satisfy her, nor tie her down. Sexy isn't the word for this man-eating goddess. Standing 5'7 inches tall, her long, beautiful, caramel colored legs lead up to a perfect size six waist. Her booty is round and sticks out like two watermelons complimenting her model-like walk of sin. Her breasts are a 38D; perky and captivating.

Just one glance will make anyone want to squeeze them just for GP (general purpose). Her long, brown hair is highlighted with beautiful blonde streaks to bring out her hazel brown eyes and compelling complexion.

Yes, Lenese has all the tools and knows how to work them. She has the ability to seduce any man without saying a word. Her eyes captivate men while inviting them subconsciously into her scheming little world. Lenese has a smile that can make the sun shine during a hurricane, and her personality is so loving and generous that it could never be ignored.

Yet, something is missing...love. Lenese is afraid of the pain that comes along with commitment. Loving the same man for ten years isn't enough when lives are too different for them to be together. Because of her Gemini characteristics, settling for just anyone is never an option. Being such a sexual creature has its pros and cons, though. Knowing her heart belongs to her ex, she uses her clients for her own sexual needs while helping them to keep their wives happy. Lenese knows it's selfish, but she doesn't give a damn.

Why not have the best of both worlds? Everyone gets what they want and she remains the best at what she does. Sex is her weapon! So, she strings guys along, teases and pleases them, but will never truly commit to any of them. She loves playing the field and having no ties or commitments. Lenese is a free spirit and no man can keep her interest long enough to hold her down.

Feeling sexy and satisfied, she struts to her full length mirror behind the office door and admires herself in this exquisite outfit. She has on a Chanel lace black see- through tank which covers a strapless black Victoria Secrets bra. No matter how much she tries, she can't resist cupping and squeezing them while moving seductively to the music in her mind.

Her fitted, denim looking Capri pants are hugging her ass like a second skin as she bounces it in the mirror like a video vixen. You will never see a panty line on her because thongs are her best friend and they feel so damn good up against her pussy piercing. The combination of the two makes her feel like she can't sit still.

She's stepping in 5 inch, black stilettos that make her calves look amazing and perfectly fit although she hates exercising. She works it out in the bedroom and her body sure does reflect it. Lenese is never the type to just lay there during sex. She loves to ride because she has total control which is usually her M.O. Every man she's ever been with has told her that she is the best, so she wears that ego like a trophy.

Lenese gives head like you can't imagine. Making love to the dick with her mouth as if it is her soul mate. Closing her eyes as she pulls it in, but opening her eyes as she slides it out. The sex faces she makes are to allure them into her while watching and feeling their excitement. Their dicks grow harder and longer with every wet, sloppy lick. She slobbers a dick down with finesse which isn't just for their benefit. That shit turns her on and her pussy gets wetter and wetter with each moan and groan.

Caressing and stroking the dick while slurping all of the saliva back into her mouth, giving it just the right amount of suction so a brief blow of air makes a slight whistling sound drives her victim crazy. She watches as their eyes roll in the back of their heads, while grabbing the back of hers. Loving the way they pull her hair back to see her face, she knows they are totally into her, and all that's left is to make them cum harder than they ever do with their wives.

Although wetness is the key, men like it to be sloppy. While watching her mouth work wonders as their dicks slip and slide in and out, up and down, and all around, they slip into her trance. She then moans and groans while gripping and slobbering all over the dicks, adding just the right mix of sensuality and consistence. Stroking it up and down as her mouth does the opposite of each motion, then putting it all in her mouth and shoving it down her throat attempting to gag on it.

This technique drives them insane because the muscles in her throat close up around the dick; squeezing it like a vagina. Then, holding it there with little or no movement as long as she can possibly stand it, they jump, move, grip, scream, squirm, and all of the above, until they "splash waterfalls" in her mouth as she gladly swallows it. Lenese feels that spitting it out will ruin the mood and this never appealed to her. She needs their undivided attention, as well as dick control at all times. Taking it all in, she then swallows while still holding them in her mouth until they fall to their knees from exhaustion and pleasure.

Chapter 2

Pleasuring Me

Lenese jumps and sits straight up in her bed to look around. Feeling a little startled, she then realizes it is just another damn nightmare.

"What the fuck?" she whispers, shaking her head and lying back down. These nightmares have been ongoing for about a month now and really affecting her mindset; not to mention her sleep. It is really weird that she doesn't remember any of the dreams and at this point it is starting to piss her off.

Lying back on her goose down pillow she finds herself butt naked with her fingers in between her legs. *There is always time.* She begins to rub gently over her clitoris that is always ready for some action. Her pussy feels wet and so warm. Her juices are running down her thighs and marinating like a steak waiting to be cooked and served. Lenese named her pussy 'Mango' because it is fat and sweet, and always juicy. It usually smells like her favorite Bath & Body Works body-wash, "Sensual Amber."

These dudes always rave about the 'wet wet' and I can see why, feeling the heat rising from 'Mango' like an inferno as soon as she opens her legs. Men lose their fucking minds when they enter her body as if they are sliding into hot lava melting with sheer delight.

They always want to cum as soon as she tightens her pussy muscles and make her walls wrap around the dick like fitted gloves. On top of that, she is a "squirter," and that is just icing on the cake. When they see her cum all over their face and dick, they go absolutely crazy like kids in a candy shop. She hasn't always been a squirter, but mastered the technique some years ago and uses it to her advantage every chance she gets. Lenese loves touching her body because it is her way of staying in tune with herself. It is second nature to her and she never thinks about it until it starts feeling so good that she wants to complete her task. Today is one of those days.

It's two hours left before getting up to head in, so she wants to make the most of her time and not waste another minute crying about these worrisome nightmares. Since she is feeling bright eyed and bushy tailed, Lenese decides to get the full enjoyment of this up and coming climax. Slowly sliding out of her king size, Barcelona canopy bed and 1200 thread count Egyptian cotton sheets, her feet finally hit the floor.

She hops up and lights up Kush flavored incense and two hazel nut candles to set her mind at ease. Then tunes into her favorite R. Kelly station, sprays her pillows and sheets with her ex's cologne (Platinum by Jay Z), and make sure her doors are locked. She reaches under her mattress and pulls out Roger (her purple dildo with rabbit ears that vibrates like nothing she's ever seen); she greets him with a smile while the anticipation of a fantastic nut makes her jittery.

As the sweet smell of Kush and hazel nut fills her room, she lays back down on her pillow, resting her eyes to clear her mind. 12 Play comes on and it is oh so perfect for this event. As R. Kelly starts counting down the ways to please his woman, Lenese starts drifting off into heaven as Roger buzzes and vibrates at the highest speed possible against her pussy lips and clit. "Um um um, damn" is all that spills from her lips as pure ecstasy and joy of her mechanical man is fulfilling her every need.

Getting ready for a spectacular climax, she moves and positions Roger in the right spot after letting him go wild all over.

No man can ever make her feel this much pleasure even while eating the pussy. Grinding back to Roger and getting ready to release what feels like the biggest nut she's ever has, "Just like a Star" by Corinne Bailey Rae comes on.

"Still I wonder why it is, I don't argue like this with anyone but you. We do it all the time, blowing out my mind……" Those few words are ringing in her head like an annoying alarm clock and she can't understand how or why her past still breaks her down emotionally.

Her whole mind set is fucked up now and the tears start flowing from her face like Niagara Falls. This song always reminds her of her ex, Antonio, and this particular moment isn't the time to cry over his ass. Feeling like she just lost her best friend, she desperately skips to the next song to regain her peace of mind. Pissed off and upset, Lenese tries to readjust and get back to where she is mentally.

"Damn him," she whispers.

He doesn't deserve my time or thoughts. Mentally struggling, she gets her train of thought back and has to reposition Roger again after dropping him to wipe the tears from her eyes. Lenese is always horny and thinking about sex, but she thinks about love more and it makes her sad whenever certain songs come on that remind her of Antonio.

Getting back to the feeling, she quickly starts grinding harder, and moving Roger in an upward and downward position while in vibration mode. As her heart beats faster and her breaths become shorter, her pussy throbs and her mind wanders off. The nut is hard and she knows her heart stopped beating because her ears are ringing and she is shaking uncontrollably.

She screams out, "Oh my God ewwwwww…yeeeesssss," clinching her teeth together until they feel like they are going to crumble apart.

"Oh how I needed that this morning," she yells. It has been almost two weeks since Roger blessed her with that feeling that always puts a huge smile on her face and forces her to drift back off into a deep sleep.

She doesn't remember any part of dreaming, nor if she even has another dream when she hears her ringtone alarm playing her favorite song, "Nothing Even Matters" by Lauren Hill urging her to get up and make a living.

Chapter 3

The Playing Ground

Dr. Stringfield is very selective about her clients. After all, she is a sex therapist and the most competitive type, but she never lets money dictate her business. Holding her appointment book and flipping to today's agenda, she realizes she has a 10 o'clock consult. Dr. Stringfield never has problems with clients liking or wanting her, but she doesn't take on a case unless they met the three requirements:

1. They have some fire left to rekindle

2. They have been married at least three years

3. They are open-minded to trying new things sexually.

The reason for these rules is to determine if they truly want their marriage to work or if they are just doing counseling to make the other person shut up about it. She's seen so many people who think they want to stay together and after wasting time, money, and energy, they end up in divorce court.

Her office is nice, cozy, and dimly lit. She always keeps lavender scented aroma therapy candles lit all over to set a relaxed mood and environment, so her clients can feel comfortable. Her nose is very sensitive and the smell of lavender helps her to wind down after a long day. She has pictures of couples intertwined in sexual positions, but in a tasteful way. These paintings are so that her clients will be comfortable with seeing others interacting sexually without feeling ashamed or disgusted.

Lenese adores art and style, which her office reflects in such a sexual way. She has a slew of fertility statues and other creations she collected on her annual retreats in different countries. Her office can put most couples in the mood from the setting alone and she loves to see how relaxed and eager they are to try anything for the sake of making their marriage work. She admires her Armani Italian leather, crème colored couch because it is soft and soothing to the touch. Just the feel of supple leather on her skin is enough to get her juices flowing and it always seems to impress her clients as well.

She remembers when Tyrone Jensen pressed her naked body up against the cold, soft leather facing forward. Her face gently against the wall and her knees sunk into the pillow-like essence as he rammed her from behind. He held her arms together at the wrist up against the wall as if she is hanging from the ceiling or a nail. Tyrone is sexy as shit and she enjoyed looking back at him while he pulled her long brown hair. He would wrap it around is fist like a rope and tame her like the wild animal she is.

The couch is complimented by a chocolate, caramel, and crème colored Persian rug which has also brought her nothing but memories of freaky and passionate sex. Like the time when Maurice Avon ate her pussy like it is Thanksgiving dinner, leaving nothing but bones. He knew exactly how to please her and his tongue feels like cotton slipping and sliding up and down the inside of her pussy lips.

He gently sucks on her clit which drives her insane, while he slides his pinky finger in her ass to heighten the experience as her juices will begin to flow significantly. Just as she is ready to cum all over his face, she feels something different that she's never feels before. It feels like she is peeing on herself. There is a lot of pressure, yet warm and enticing.

After it is over, she can't feel her legs as Maurice laid his head on her inner thigh; his face covered with her silky white cum. "You just squirted all over me," he said looking surprised. That is a first for her and she enjoyed it oh so well. After a few times of doing this with Maurice, she'd learned to master the technique and can "squirt" on cue.

She loves the finer things in life and she surely can afford them, especially because she doesn't have children. Lenese always dreams of having children, but she wants them with the right man. Hell, she is only twenty-nine and not thinking of settling down or having any kids.

Trusting men is never an option because she knows from experience that all of them cheat. Dr. Stringfield has slept with over seventy five percent of her clients and doesn't need any assistance persuading the men to be with her. She uses her sex appeal to train the men on how to treat and thoroughly make love to their wives. Although the wives will ever know what she is doing, their loving husbands are more than willing to get any type of sexual instruction the seductive doctor suggest or offers.

The couples have to sign a 90 day contract which guarantees better sex lives in twelve sessions or less for clients being seen weekly. The first four sessions consist of seeing the couple as a whole. Next, there are six alternating weeks of private sessions with the wives and husbands separately. Lastly, she uses the final 2 weeks to make sure the couple are on the same track and ecstatic about their new sexual relationship with their spouses.

Her technique is to see what their issues with one another are and if they relate to infidelity, low self-esteem or just boredom. In all her years she's found that financial issues are hardly ever the problem because she is in high demand and very expensive. But, in some cases, one of the two spends outrageously, leaving the other to handle all the consequences.

So, when it is financial, the therapist makes sure to let them know that they have to get that part of their issue handled before she can help them. Then, she helps them build a mentally sexual appetite for one another by role playing and pulling sexual thoughts, desires, and ideas from deep fantasies.

An easy exercise is exotic and erotic massages that start at the head and end up with the toes. Showing the wives how to stroke their husband's dicks from the nuts to the head in a slow, circular motion brings excitement as well as hands on training. The easiest trick is to grip it at the bottom of the shaft and glide their hand gently up to the head then back down again, which leaves the men feeling wanted and horny.

Lenese has toys for days and loves to experiment with all types of scented massage and body oils. She even offers videos in certain sessions to show "how to" or "how not to" do things during their sexual escapades. Dr. Stringfield uses any means necessary to make these couples sexually attracted and satisfied with one another again. It motivates her as well as satisfies her own desires of having "the perfect relationship."

Chapter 4

Man of The Hour

Just as Lenese is looking down at her Rolex diamond watch, Liz (her loyal assistant) buzzes her on her intercom and announces that Janard and Enga Tremell are waiting while sliding their file through the slot on the back of Dr. Springfield's office door. She always request that each couple bring a wedding photo (preferably full body) to attach it to their file which keeps them focused on how happy they are at that particular moment in their lives. She also requests a full medical history which has to be accurate and up to date so she knows up front if her clients have any medical conditions that can counteract with sexual positions and/or situations.

Quickly opening the file to read a little background before inviting her potential clients in, her jaws drop and a little drool falls from her bottom lip. Slurping the slobber back into her mouth, she thinks *God damn Janard is fine as hell.* He stood about 6'3 with jet black hair that is neatly cut. His strong features include a sharp jaw with high cheek bones that enhance his buttery bronze skin tone. His eyebrows are thick just like his hair.

Those ocean green eyes slant upward just a little bit and look as if they will jump off the page the way they are piercing out at her. Janard's nose is semi-pointed and his face falls into a perfectly curved chin. He has a thin build which is perfect for his height, but he still has muscles that are easily noticed through his midnight blue, Versace shirt. Instantly she pictures herself jumping up in his arms and riding him as if he is a horse in the Kentucky Derby; as he stands there palming her perfectly round ass ever so abruptly.

"Focus," she caught herself saying out loud while analyzing Enga as if sizing up the competition.

What in the world is going on with her today? *First, it was this crazy ass dream and now I'm acting like this woman stole my damn man.* Enga is absolutely gorgeous. She is 5'11 with long, perfectly shaped legs that you can see through the slit in her beautifully custom-made wedding gown.

She looks to be around one hundred and fifty pounds or so, which is perfect for her height. She has long, blonde, naturally curly hair that stops about mid back and is common for Swedish women.

Unlike most Caucasian women, she has curves that can cause an accident and if Lenese were gay, she will definitely be her type. Her eyes are the clearest of blue that Lenese has ever seen and her eyelashes are "Cover Girl" long and thick. Her lips are even stunning as if she has some collagen work done and looks as though there are perfectly polished with shimmery, pink gloss. Her cheeks are high, but amazingly accent her facial structure.

She looked as though she is a perfect "C" cup and has no waist what so ever. She is naturally beautiful and again Lenese feels some type of way without even knowing her personally. It is something about the photo which leads her to feel that this marriage is definitely in trouble. Enga's eyes tell a story that Lenese isn't sure she will ever know.

"Pull it together," she says to herself as she opens her office door and invites the Tremells' in. As they stand to their feet, she thinks, *Wow! They look like they just stepped out of a magazine.* Lenese is unsure of which one did the cheating, but deep down inside, she is praying it is Janard. He walks with such confidence and swag and smells like lust.

She feels herself getting weak at the knees as he gently brushes past her in the doorway of her office. *Oh my God, my panties are soaked.* Feeling eager to sit down and rub her legs together so she can enjoy the moisture between her thighs while daydreaming about Janard slurping up all of her juices as she smothers him. Enga, however, briskly walks past her like Martha Stewart, reeking of Liz Claiborne, as if in a hurry to get this show on the road.

Lenese escorts them to her favorite couch, tells them to make themselves at home, and offers a glass of wine to help them unwind. Moscato is her favorite, but she has other kinds as well. She wants to make sure their minds are in a subtle place before they embark on this journey with her. They accept the gesture, settle back and exhale.

She doesn't shake hands to introduce herself because she finds that to be more formal and that isn't the atmosphere she wants to create. She takes a different approach. "What do you know about me and why did you choose me?" she asks softly, being careful not to kill the mood while sipping on her own glass of much needed wine.

Expecting Enga to pour her anxious looking heart out, Lenese is surprised to hear the sweet Barbadian baritone of Janard's voice say "I just want to make LOVE to my wife again," as he shifts his body to the edge of the couch. At that very moment, Lenese knows that Enga is the problem…she means the cheater!

Chapter 5

Cheating Ain't Easy

Lenese isn't sure how to handle this situation with the Tremells' because she has never been this attracted to one of her clients. They just left and she can't put their file down or stop staring and smiling to herself, looking at Janard in the photo. He is so perfect inside and out.

Lenese spent the last hour listening to him cry about how Enga cheated on him and how he will do anything for her while she just sat there with no remorse. *What the hell is wrong with this woman? He is caring, thoughtful, sexy, handsome, and giving; a good provider.* He is a pilot and Enga is a flight attendant which explained how they met.

Lenese starts feeling the temperature rise in the room as she pictures Janard Tremell in his uniform. She can't believe that she is actually sweating between her thighs, breasts, and down her back. *What the hell is going on here?*

She's never feels this clammy about any man besides her ex and she can't understand it. This beautiful young doctor met men all the time, but no one has ever affected her like Janard.

When he opened his mouth to speak, she wants to melt like a pop cycle on the 4th of July. If Enga hasn't been in the session, Lenese knew she will have attacked his vulnerable side and fucked the shit out of him…tears and all. She wants him oh so badly and her pussy is throbbing as she imagines how he will cry out her name with passion while she is on top of him moving forwards and back again in a rowing motion.

Lenese pictures the look of agony on his face as she grinds down hard on his dick as if she is digging with a shovel. She becomes chest to chest with him while doing this so she can feel his hot breath on her face...staring in his beautiful eyes. Then she gently brushes against his lips with hers, just enough to entice him, but not surrendering to a kiss. After that she gently licks the top and bottom of his lips in a counter clockwise motion as if she are licking her own, knowing that kissing him will make him cum faster and making this last as long as possible.

She knows how to move her tongue in ways that men cannot resist. Kissing is her passion and she only shares this with men she cares about. No other client has the privilege of feeling her lips on theirs, although many have tried. Maybe it sounds crazy or even backwards because she doesn't mind giving head, but that is just sex and Lenese knows how to separate feelings from JUST sex.

Lenese can't explain why, but something deep down inside of her wants more than just sex with Janard. She wants to make love to Janard and treat him the way he deserves to be treated. Lenese wants to wrap her legs around him and never let him go. *What the fuck is wrong with me? How can I make love to someone I don't love....or do I? Is this what love at first sight feels like?* These thoughts cloud her mind like the sky on a rainy day.

Is this man brought to me in this situation, under these circumstances in disguise? Am I really supposed to try to help them with their marriage or am I supposed to help them see that it can't be saved and latch on to him for myself? Lenese is feeling more and more uncomfortable with every thought of seeing them together again. It almost feels like butterflies or as if she is going to vomit.

"This shit ain't healthy," speaking out loud and shaking her head. Lenese knows she has to switch up the way she usually handles the sessions and just see them on a one-on-one basis to start so she can really get down to the Nitti gritty and find out if Janard is worth pursuing. Knowing she is wrong for the thoughts about her new client, but everything happens for a reason and she is going to try to follow her heart this time instead of her head to see where it leads.

As she puts the file down and opens her schedule book, she buzzes Liz to call the Tremells' and let them know that the next appointment is not going to be a couples appointment. Instead, she wants to just see Enga and go from there. Lenese keeps flashing back to how unhappy Janard looked and how he is so persistent about making things better between him and Enga. He just kept saying that he wants a family and she doesn't, and that he feels she just wants him for sex. Lenese knows now that this really messed with his performance because his heart is broken and his feelings are in the way.

He explained how he can't stop picturing her with "someone else" and how sex is just sex for him. Janard explained that he and Enga has a deal that they will start having kids once they has been married for five years and has their finances in order, but she reneged on the deal.

She will just say things like "I'm just not ready," "We should wait 'till we're older," or "I don't think I will be good with kids." That last statement bothered Lenese because most of the time when a woman says that, she doesn't want kids at all and she feels like Enga is misleading Janard which will later end their marriage. Although Lenese it isn't her place to speak on her thoughts of this in front of Janard, she wants to so badly. Instead, she needs to have some one-on-one time with Enga and really find out if she's trying to save her marriage or if she is there because Janard wants to save it. Enga doesn't seem to be in love with Janard either, but then again, maybe she isn't a person who wears her emotions on her sleeve as he does.

Enga's reasoning for cheating is because they always argued about having children right before sex and it is a major turn off. *What is her fucking problem? This bitch has it all: a fine ass husband who is a good provider and seems to be very open and honest.* At that very moment she knew that Enga doesn't appreciate what she has and soon and very soon, she won't have to worry about it anymore.

Chapter 6

Roger Gets None

Pulling up to her Condo on 34th and Peachtree, Lenese yelps at the sight of a burgundy Beamer in her garage. "What the fuck did I tell this chic? I'm really gonna need my damn key back," fussing to herself. She struts her cute ass up the steps to her front door, pushing it open because it isn't even closed all the way, and screams,   "D' Juanaaaaaaaaaa!! Didn't I tell your ass about parking in my mother fuckin garage bitch?"

Her sister trots down the stairs (trying to hide a couple pair of heels and some jewelry behind her back) laughing at her big sister with a smile so big and pretty that it looks like her teeth are sparkling. D'Juana is Lenese's baby sister and has a smile so inviting that she can't help but smile back at this bitch.

D'Juana is 24 years old and model-type pretty. She stands about 5'8 and walks as if she is Naomi Campbell, Eva Pigford or somebody who gets paid for walking. Her skin tone is of Hershey chocolate complexion, just smooth and brown. Her eyes slant-like an Asian and are the darkest chestnut brown you will ever see.

D'Juana's hair is long and comes just under her shoulders but wraps around her face like it has been raked into place. Her lips are big and have the perfect "McDonald's Arch" shape. So, when she puts her lip gloss on, she looks like she can sell America to the richest man out there.

She is slim, but shaped perfectly, wearing a 34 C cup and a perfect size six. Lenese looks at D'Juana thinking how much she looks like herself when she is that age. Shaking her head and walking towards her to meet her half way, Lenese holds out her arms to welcome her little sister with a big hug and kiss on the lips as if she hasn't seen her in years.

"Damn bitch, you act like I didn't just see your ass yesterday," D'Juana complained, as she turned and walked back up towards her sister's bedroom; being careful to keep the items hidden.

"What are you doing here nicca?" she asks as she kicks off her 5 inch stilettos and flops down on her bed: falling to one arm and tucking it under her chin.

"Let's go out tonight chic!" D'Juana yelled falling onto the bed beside her.

Two hours have passed and D'Juana is long gone as Lenese finally removes herself from her pillow top mattress and hits the power button on her 50 inch flat screen LED/3D television that hangs from her ceiling. She'd gotten caught up watching 106 and Park on BET and doesn't notice the time slipping away from her.

Her favorite rapper, Jay Z, is on the show today as she *reminisced* about their meeting after one of his concerts. She and Jay are good friends and he's invited her to come by his club anytime where he will make sure she is treated like royalty. She thinks, *We are going to the 40/40 club tonight to meet some ballers, get drunk, party and bull shit like only we knew how to do.*

Lenese walks over to her marble Jacuzzi, jet tub to run a bath with her favorite Bath and Body Works "Jasmine Vanilla Aroma Therapy" bath scrub oil. As the sweet smell begins to fill the air, Lenese starts preparing for her bath by setting the ambiance. She lights some Issey Miyake incense tonight because the smell mixes so well with the scent of the bath oil.

She also lights about 5 candles that are set up all around the tub, and stops the running water. She watches as the steam from the hot bath fogs the mirrors that are covering every inch of wall in her bathroom. All that's missing is Roger.

Lenese places Roger on the side of the tub as she tunes into Plies radio on Pandora. Tonight she wants to feel extra sexy and irresistible so who better to listen to then Plies describing every ounce of what sexy is to men. Lenese feels like he is talking directly to her because she knows she is the shit.

She is pretty, intelligent, financially independent and stable, sexy, hood, and strong all in one. Lenese thinks of herself as boujie and ghetto so she often refers to herself as boujhetto! Not to mention, her personality is as high strung as a beach blonde Barbie- type.

Yes, she has it all and she is only missing one thing...a man. She misses those strong hands gripping her closely; that manly smell that keeps her wet; that feeling of security just knowing he will be there through thick and thin to love and protect her. Lenese wants Janard and she is going to have him.

As Plies starts' telling her that he only thinks of her on two occasions and that's, when he wants or needed it; Lenese starts feeling herself emotionally and literally. The sexy mistress slides the spaghetti string straps off her pecan shoulders like a man will...ever so gently and softly. Once the straps are off, the rest of the clothes slide off her body as if it are silk and falls lightly onto her marble floor. Lenese steps carefully into the hot bath and lets her body sink down until the water grabs her stomach and feels like fire on her skin. Jumping and whispering,

"Oooohhhh," as she starts moving more slowly down into the steaming hot bath.

She can't risk the water burning her nipples so she lifts her hands, bringing them up her stomach and grabs her voluptuous breasts to let the heat of the water prepare them for full exposure. Once settled in the water and her perky D's are floating like water balloons, she sticks out her thick but long tongue until it slightly touches her breasts.

Licking them like a Popsicle, stroking them from bottom to top as far as her tongue will reach so the water runs down the side of her face with every stroke. She grabs them like oranges and squeezes passionately to bring more of them into her mouth as her nose is embedded between all the cleavage.

Slowly, her right hand slides down to her belly button as she imagines Janard touching her with his own fingers. Closing her eyes and caressing her titties with her left hand, she finds her prize and begins massaging it without thinking twice about it. In her mind, Janard is sliding his fingers across her pussy lips and clit in a circular, up and down motion.

As she moans and groans, she feels his fingers slide into her hole and fondles her insides as if he is playing in Jell-O. Her insides feel warm to the touch and wraps around his finger like it belongs there. Lenese knew then how much she wants him because she hates insertion of anything besides dick and she rarely lets anyone touch her clit unless they are preparing to eat it. As his finger slides in and out of her, she grows even hornier.

Picturing him standing over her with his shirt off, showing that six-pack that she knows he has, with sweat trickling down his chest and stomach from the steam, she almost loses it. His fingers feel like heaven as they find her G spot and she knows she isn't going to need Roger tonight. Lenese starts grinding harder and twirling her ass around like the spin cycle of a washing machine. Feeling that familiar tingling feeling, she realizes this experience is about take her into nonexistence.

Although the music is still playing, she can't hear a thing because her ears feel like they are going to pop from being in a tunnel or on a plane. "Oooohh," she moans and groans, as Janard's fingers feel like they are all over and inside her pussy going a thousand miles an hour like Roger does.

Taking a breath so deep that her body freezes up, she feels her feet pointing straight out like someone is stretching her entire body. Her heart stops beating and her eyes roll in the back of her head as she screams out "I love you Janard!" She can't even pull it together as she lies there shaking and sweating, feeling like she just ran 5 miles.

Finally opening her eyes, she realizes that she fingered herself and came. *What the fuck just happened? I've never done that before,* she thinks realizing she is in deep trouble because Janard stays on the brain and she won't be able to control her feelings much longer.

Chapter 7

Party and Bull Shit

As Lenese pulls up in front of the 40/40 Club, she is greeted by Justin, the valet guy, ready and waiting to take the keys to her all black Range Rover Limited Edition with all black rims and a touch of chrome on the spokes. The interior is all black to match and so are the soft leather seats.

This is her dream vehicle and she makes sure to let Justin know, "Don't be doing donuts in my baby," with a look on her face that means business.

Winking at Justin, she hands him the keys as he opens her door. As soon as she steps out of the truck, heads begin to turn making her feel as if she is a celebrity. Eating it up and twisting a little harder, she walks around to the side where D'Juana and Liz are waiting impatiently.

"Damn chic! What? You has to work your magic on the youngin' to get your prize possession parked just right. D'Juana says sarcastically, turning the corner of her lips up and smirking at him all at the same time.

As usual, Lenese knows she is killing them with the all-white spaghetti string (that tied around her neck), fitted dress that comes about 2 inches above her knees. The dress has diamond accented sparkles in it and the entire back is out, falling into a V-shape right above her plump ass. The front only has enough material to cover her nipples, as it also slopes down in a V-Shape.

It is dressed up with her platinum and diamond necklace and matching bracelet, earrings, and watch that Antonio had custom made especially for her birthday last year. Antonio introduced her to the finer things in life long before he decided to disappear from it.

Although she doesn't care to be reminded of him, she can't think of anything more appropriate for this special occasion. *Hell, I am on the VIP guest list at my celebrity friend's new club and what better way to show my appreciation than to bless them all with some sexy hot chocolate?*

Lenese exhales as she secretly pats herself on the back for making a name for herself and living her life like it is golden. If only her daddy could see her now.

She knows he would be so proud. Well, not for the things she does with her practice, but just because she's following her dreams and doesn't take "no" for an answer. Her dad passed in a car accident when Lenese is only seventeen and although it is one of the most tragic memories of her life, it taught her to be self- sufficient….independent.

Her five inch platinum stilettos are even embroidered with diamonds across the top and around the heels. They are also a gift, but not from Antonio. These came from Malcolm, a completely satisfied client who is a successful Stock Broker from New York. He and his lovely wife came all the way to Atlanta to seek her services because they heard "Lenese is the best."

After a few sessions with Malcolm, he swears he is in love, just not with his wife. He starts buying her gifts, proclaiming his love and carrying on about starting over. Lenese directed him back to his wife, taught her how to fuck the shit out of her husband, and closed their file.

Lenese shakes her head while holding it high, taking each stair down like a fallen mountain. Knowing that every man she'd ever sexed wants more than just sex with her is a compliment, still she will never fall for their attempts. The first rule of business is, if he will cheat on his wife with you, he will definitely cheat on you.

Lenese pinned up her hair for this occasion to reveal her tattoo of about 50 beautifully colored stars that begins at the crack of her ass and zigzags up her back to come across her right shoulder. This symbolizes her starting from the bottom, reaching for the stars, and making it to the top. Lenese is certainly feeling the atmosphere and somebody's son is going to find out just how much tonight. She is in the mood for hot, steamy sex, and her eyes are scanning the line while walking straight pass everyone.

Guard, there is no need to announce herself, as Jay left special instructions for her and makes sure they know who she is. D'Juana and Liz are right behind her as usual, sopping up all of the stares and dirty looks everyone is giving them for cutting the line. These two are used to this whenever they go anywhere with Lenese. After all, they have been best friends since middle school, and Liz is two years older than D'Juana.

Liz is a Boricua or as the fellas say, a Puerto Rican chica. Pretty isn't the word for this 26 year old single mom who started her medical internship for Lenese almost a year ago. She is 5'9 with a buttery, toffee skin tone. Her long, coal black locks fall down to her slightly purged bootie.

Liz's hips are wide and sexy, drawing more attention than she wants at times. Her bra size has to be around a 34B and her stomach is as flat as an ironing board. These two together are double trouble, but always have each other's back, and oh how they love going out with Lenese because she knows everyone and VIP status is never a question. A cute, young hostess escorts the ladies upstairs to a VIP booth Jay set up for them. The secluded hideout is an all glass enclosure and the gorgeous trio can look down and see everything and everyone.

"Now this is what the fuck I'm talking 'bout" D'Juana said reaching for a wine glass off the table that is sitting next to three bottles of Louis Roederer Cristal Rose, chilling on ice.

The skybox has about five flat screen monitors hanging from the ceilings showing videos and basketball games. The monitor closest to the Royal blue sectional, plush leather sofa that seems like it wrapped around the box, shows what is happening on the other side of the club.

"Sweeeet! Jay sure knows how to do it big." Liz chuckles while shaking her head and grabbing a glass of her own.

"He sure does....in more ways than you know. Lenese mumbles quickly turning her head to see if D'Juana heard her and what the hell her smart ass mouth is gonna say. Although D'Juana caught the comment, she doesn't entertain it.

She just hands Lenese a glass and says, "Stop fantasizing and pop this bottle Cameron Diaz style like What Happens in Vegas!"

Whistling and coaching, smiling and yelling, the pair finally convince Lenese to do the trick she learned from Cameron D., which (by the way) only took her a week to master. As Lenese cut the top off the bottle sideways with Champaign spilling out like a waterfall, she notices a man in all black staring up at her.

His sexy ass is standing about 6'2 inches tall and looks to be about 200 pounds. He is wearing black shades with diamond studs all around the lenses. His coal black hair lay thick and wavy on his perfectly shaped head. His line-up is tighter then a dick in the butt and his goatee is shaped up just right.

He has them dark, smooth, weed- smoking lips that look like they are placed on his face by an artist. She can't help but notice the big ass diamond studs in both ears that seem to be the size of green peas. He is also wearing a long, platinum chain with an Eagle as the charm that (to Lenese) resembles freedom and independence and hangs down to his mid area. *Um um um,* Lenese thinks to herself as she begins undressing him with her eyes. *Finally, some eye candy,* she tosses her hair to the other side.

She never takes her eyes off this prize as it won't be so easy if she tried. He is rockin' an all-black Roca Wear starter jacket with his face embroidered in diamonds on the back. *This Negro loves himself.* It covers a nice black T-shirt and black jeans that sag just enough not to be noticed, but not too much to hug his nuts either. She can see the bulge in his pants and is very impressed, as she wonders if it is an all-natural bulge or induced by her own amazing appearance... feeling herself. Dude is leaning up against a pole by a bar with one foot cocked; heal up, as if he's been watching her for a while.

Her hands start sweating when she peeps a grin come across his manly shaped face and a glimpse of hope jumping in his deep brown eyes after removing his shades.

"Helloooooooooo," D'Juana sings while hitting her glass with a fork to steal back her sister's attention from whatever guy she is drooling over, with her mouth wide open.

"Can we get some alcohol pleeeaaase," D'Juana said still singing the words.

"Oh, my bad," Lenese quickly replies while looking a bit disturbed. Right then D'Juana whines, "Who are you looking at anyway?" as she turns back to the direction that has kept her sister occupied for

Lenese starts whispering things like "I miss you papi! "I know you want this! Ooohh daddy, punish me with the stopper! I've been a bad girl!"

Suddenly this love-sick woman drops to her knees as she pulls and yanks at his belt buckle feeling as if she can't get them loose fast enough. Antonio starts helping her, laughing out loud and staring in her eyes because he remembers he taught her very well.

Antonio is her first everything! He taught her how to ride and how to take it from the back. He taught her how to suck a mean dick and he hated the fact that any other nigga got the pleasure of finding out how the love of his life got down and dirty!

"Slow down bae," he demands.

Lenese said, "Fuck this buckle and shit," and slid his semi- baggy jeans down while they are still fastened.

Antonio loves when Lenese takes control and rapes him, so to speak. She is the only woman who can get his engine roaring and make him feel like he will cum before he even starts. He loves when she talks dirty to him, yanking and pulling on his dick, especially when she acts like she can't get enough.

Most of all, he cherishes her lips, with or without gloss. He appreciates her natural beauty and often tells her she doesn't need to wear makeup. He loves staring into her eyes as if he lost something long ago and is searching for it through her eyes. Whenever he feels like this, he knows he wants to make love to this magnificent woman standing before him and not just fuck her like she is some bitch off the streets.

Right then, Antonio leans forward and tucks his hands under her arms and pulls her up to be face to face with him. Even though she has on 5 inch heels, she is still shorter than him and that shit turns her on even more. She feels like a dog in heat once the smell of his damn cologne enters her nose. He grabs the back of her neck and slowly pulls her towards him, planting a firm, but gentle kiss on her lips. *Oh, no he didn't,* she thinks, enjoying the warmth of his lips pressing up against her own.

As his tongue enters her mouth (feeling like heaven), she melts in his arms feeling the life just leave her body. She is glad his other hand is on the nape of her back to stop her from plunging straight back like the old Lipton ice tea commercials. She swears the kiss lasted every bit of ten minutes or more. It feels like he is making love to her soul through her mouth. She can't understand why and how this man has this effect on her and why can't he just do right?

"We really need to talk bae," Antonio suggest in a loving, but firm voice.

"I know, but let's not ruin the moment," Lenese whispers.

"You might regret this in the morning Lovie," he says slowly, pulling her closer to him.

"I will never regret sexing you up," she moans, wanting to fall backwards all over again feeling his tight grip around her extremely horny body.

"I won't be here with you tomorrow and YOU made it very clear that you don't want to be with me remember?" he reminds her, staring dead in her eyes.

Although Lenese knows she should be more attentive, she can't help but notice his breath always smells so clean, cool, and minty. *Why oh why is everything about this man so perfect for me?*

"I want you, but I want you forever and you can't promise me forever. You can't promise me that you won't get arrested or killed tonight. Hell, you won't even get a bodyguard because you feel your reputation is enough to get you through!" she cries out with a look of grief and concern upon her face.

"Bae, you know how I roll! I'm not a celebrity or the President, so what do I need a bodyguard for? I can guard my own body and yours if you let me. I believe that everything happens for a reason and when The Man Upstairs is ready for me, I'm going to be ready for Him!" He demands in a calm, cool, and collective voice that ate right through Lenese.

How is this nigga always so laid back, living life like he doesn't have a care in the world? She can't understand it. All she knows is she wants to be with him more than life itself, but he won't submit, so neither will she.

What do you want from me then, Antonio?" speaking through her left cheek. "Why do you tease and torment me this way? You keep showing up just to leave me all over again. I can't keep putting myself through this!

"I hate you so much for not being there for me like you promised you always will be." Lenese cries while the tears are falling beyond her control now.

"Bae, I've always been there when you needed me. I'm here now. I will never leave your side if you just take me as I am," he says in a reassuring tone. "I have always put you on a pedestal and put no other woman before you. You are my queen, Lovie. You know this!" he states, proclaiming his unconditional love for her.

Still that isn't enough for Lenese. "You know me better than anyone else in my life and you know that I want what I want," Antonio says, standing his ground.

"Well, I can't wake up to that phone call or knock at the door," Lenese replies, shaking her head and pulling away from him. Antonio wipes the tears from her lovely face while telling her just how much he loves her. This just makes her cry harder. Then, she falls to the couch in the restroom, covering her face, sobbing out loud (now), and shaking her head.

"Just go Antonio!" she cries softly feeling like her world just came to an end. "Just go!"

At that very moment, as always seeming to be a message from above, ExFactor by Lauren Hill comes on and Lenese runs into a stall because she knows she's going to lose it and that her night is ruined. The words are burning the pit of her stomach because they fit their relationship so perfectly.

"It can all be so simple, but you'd rather make it hard. Loving you is like a battle, and we both end up with scars. Tell me, who I have to be to get some reciprocity?

No one loves you more than me, and no one ever will!" After knowing this guy most of her life, she can't get past the life she'd always known him to have. Wanting so badly for him to just grow up and get a real job so they can live happily ever after, yet, knowing deep down in her heart that he will never last in the "white or blue collared" world. This man has never been a follower and to give in to her meant giving up on himself, which will only cause resentment for them both down the line.

Lenese tries desperately to ignore the words of the song, but they are piercing her ears and demanding her attention once again:

"I keep letting you back in...How can I explain myself? As painful as this thing has been, I just can't be with no one else. See, I know what we got to do; you let go and I'll let go too. 'Cause no one's hurt me more than you, and no one ever will!"

Antonio knows there is no talking to her now, so he turns around and leaves the oversized bathroom. She then leaves about five minutes later after getting her makeup and emotions together.

Lenese walks over to her sister and assistant with a look on her face that says, "Don't even ask." so they don't. Instead, Liz hands her a glass and posts up her own for a toast.

"Live, Love, and Learn." she smiles and blurts out as all three of these single, beautiful, successful women click their glasses together and take their drinks to the head for the first time tonight.

"I thought I was going to have to come get that ass; making us wait to toast and drink. Have you lost your mind woman? We came here to party and bull shit, remember? Now, let's do the damn thing!" D'Juana yells out loud prancing her slim, but fine ass towards the extremely full dance floor. While grabbing the hands of her two best friends, and leading them out onto the dance floor because, "No Hands" (by Wacka Flaka) comes on and she knows it is her sister's jam. As the three amigos fall into the crowd landing themselves between men dancing all around them, they believe tonight will be one to remember.

"Party, party, party…let's all get wasted! Liz screams as they twist and turn, laugh and giggle, bump and grind, and enjoy themselves like it is their birthday. Lenese doesn't even look for Antonio anymore that night. She just wants to drink her blues away and wake up tomorrow like HE never even happened.

Chapter 9

A Helluva Apology

"Mmmmm. Yes. That's it, right there. Ahhh. Ummm hmmm," Lenese moans and groans, squirming and moving her hips in a circular motion like she is hula hooping. "Damnnnn, you know what I need. Do that shit lover," she whispers. Grabbing the back of his head, she pulls him deeper into the wetness that he's created with his long, thick, warm, and delicate tongue.

His strokes are long and very soft. He licks from bottom to top as he makes his tongue point and curve just right when reaching her exquisite clit. She hears him moan with enjoyment of feeling her try to break away from his grasp. Then, he grabs her clit with his teeth ever so carefully and slurps on it like a straw, thirsty for her juices.

Oh my God, she thinks, as this man goes straight to her 'G Spot' like he has navigation on his fuckin' tongue. He is using his lips to massage her clit while his tongue is slightly touching it, which absolutely drives Lenese nuts. This man knows her oh too well, and it scares her because for once, she is not in control.

Lenese pushes his shoulders back with both hands and squeezes his face between her thighs, but this doesn't do anything to help. In fact it feels as if he got stimulated and makes his tongue move in a vibrating motion. If she doesn't know better, she will have sworn it is a bullet on her pussy.

This man has skillz that she can't fuck with and definitely can't ignore. His tongue slides inside Mango and goes on a search as if it is mutha fuckin Jacques Cousteau. As Lenese opens her legs up and grabs her toes, straightening her legs out, doing a half split in the air; her legs fall in a V shape. She wants to help him reach his sunken treasure so she pulls them apart to a 90 degree angle so his face can get no interference and he has straight pussy to enjoy.

Knowing he is impressed because she feels his nose slide down, tickling her clit as this man is sucking her insides out. "Oh my fucking God," she screams out as she feels that tingly feeling signifies squirting ahead. He is moving his head in an up and down motion like rowing a boat and all she can do is grab the edge of the bed and hold on for this amazing ride.

Just when Lenese is about to arrive at her final destination, this man wraps his arms around her knees, grabs them firmly, and yanks her ass down to the edge of the bed where he is kneeling. *Shit, I like that.* He pushes her legs straight up and holds them both with one hand close by her ankles as she struggles to get her eyes open and see what he is about to do with his other hand.

Lenese is anxious to feel him inside of her with all the force that he uses to pull her closer. She loves that rough shit and it turns her on when a man does it just right...with confidence and caress at the same time. She doesn't know where she is and doesn't even care.

She loves to fuck and Mango is extremely juicy tonight because this man is eating the shit out of her; leaving her bursting with cum that lasts as long as the Nile River runs. And to be totally honest, this shit feels so good and real to her that she doesn't even want to open her eyes, in fear of it being just another dream. So she just keeps them closed and basks in her own juices desperately awaiting her opponent's next move.

Right then she feels pressure at the entrance of Mango and it feels delicious. Being a freak has its rewards and challenges. However, the pressure grows into pain as this familiar, massive dick forces entry into her honeycomb hideout. "Goddamnnnnnn," falls from her lips in pure pain and pleasure. Lenese can feel every curve, every vein; every inch of the dick slowly sliding into her walls, burning as if her inner layer of skin is being scraped off.

Yet, the wetness of Mango saves her from screaming out with agony. This seductive man knows what he is doing because every time Lenese locks her pussy muscles around his dick strokes his dick sideways, making her feel extreme ecstasy while Mango's wetness runs down his dick.

"Ahhhh," he groans with relief. Right then she feels his other hand palm her ass cheek firmly. His intensions are to guide his manhood in more perfectly, pulling out for a quick second which feels like an eternity as she unleashes the sheets. To her surprise, he slides it back in with so much passion while filling her up inside and leaving her speechless.

What the fuck is going on here? Where is my control, and why is he giving me the business like this? Lenese keeps asking herself over and over again in her mind as if she doesn't already know. This dude is acting like he has something to prove, but she isn't complaining at all. *Wait a minute; am I cuming on this dick already?*

Oh damn, he is going to knock my back wall down. Lenese digs her fingernails into his butt cheeks, grabbing and pulling him closer so he can go deeper. Again to her surprise, he IS going deeper and she realizes that every inch of the dick is not inside of her just yet. He pushes her legs back to her head until they touch the headboard, moving inside her with intensity.

Once he is on top of her and his entire manhood is inside of her, Lenese feels his cool breath on her neck as his lips kiss it all over; sucking and making smacking noises. Feeling his face turn to hers as he then whispers in a voice she's been longing to hear "Open your eyes and look at me bae!" But, she doesn't want to open her eyes to see Antonio's gorgeous fucking face again, tonight.

He finally releases her legs from the grip he has mastered and they fall right into place, wrapping around his waist. "Ooohhh your pussy feels sooo good wrapped around this dick," he whispers as he comes in and out of it with long, slow strokes. Antonio is making love to her soul as he starts to kiss her so passionately that she feels like this is a movie and she is the leading lady.

Damn, her pussy is getting wetter while 'the show stopper' grows bigger. Lenese just wants to enjoy tonight and not think about tomorrow, so she emotionally puts her feelings aside and begins grinding back on the dick so hard that her ass leaves the bed. He starts losing control and pulls out so fast she believes he is about to cum, but he doesn't.

Instead, he flips her over like a pancake and pulls her up to her knees. He places his left hand on her stomach (as he always does) and slaps her ass with 'the stopper' just likes she likes it. He uses the head to play around the pussy hole, making her hornier and wetter, even wetter. As her juices start running, he slowly slides his massiveness in until only his nuts hang out and her stomach muscles tense up in his hand.

"I can't take it baby," she moans, but he can't stop. He knows she loves it and how she wants it. Antonio pushes her face down in the pillow and holds the back of her neck so she can't move it. Although the shit hurts like a bitch, Lenese isn't going out like that. She twists and turns her head loose from his grasp and looks back at him with her mouth wide open, gasping for air and moaning with delight.

He pounds the pussy harder because he can't resist the 'look back'! "What you tryna prove babe?" she cries, tooting her ass up further all at the same time. It feels like he is stroking her pelvic bone as her insides are shifting positions. "Damn you know how to give it to me. You got this shit on lock! What the fuck you tryna do? I don't want no more babe....I promise!" She hollers.

She notices this only makes matters worse as Antonio gives her short but hard strokes. This shit is

making her cum instantly and she can't help but cry out, "You're the fuckin best papi! Do that shit daddy! Oooohh papi, I love this dick.
The…show...stopper...ain't playing is he?" At that moment, she arches the fuck out of her back which makes him go insane.

He loses his mutha fuckin' mind and tries to put his dick through her, only hurting himself in the process because all the blood rushes through his dick to the head and he can't hold back any longer. With his face changing shapes and colors, he yells out, "FUUUCCCKK.......!" Then, he drops to his side, rolling off her and onto his back, lying spread out, and breathing hard as hell. Lenese smiles looking at him and says "Is that all you got?"

Chapter 10

Reminiscing

The next morning, Lenese pulls up at her office around 10:45 and scans the parking lot as she always does. There is a private entrance in the back to her office and she loves it because she can slide in and out without anyone knowing. Her appointment with Enga isn't for another 30 minutes so she has time to relax after being in traffic for the last 20 minutes. Although she enjoys working in Atlanta, the commute is a bit much.

Lenese is really feeling herself today after fucking Antonio's brains out last night, although she can't remember how she got home. Her last memory is taking shots of Patron with the girls and dancing exotically in front of the mirrors on the back wall.

All she knows is that she is glad she doesn't take that key from Antonio or change her alarm pass code. She really needed that from him last night, especially after seeing him and having the short conversation they had. She needed to know she would always be his first concern, even if she isn't his first priority.

Reminiscing about the night before, she starts having flash backs of the 'Sexcapades' they shared, and her pussy got hot all over again. Feeling a bit feverish, she notices her palms are sweating as she grips the steering wheel a little harder. "How does he do that shit?" she catches herself speaking out loud. Oh how Antonio can eat the pussy better than anyone she's ever dealt with. Lenese isn't sure if it is because she is in love with him or his skills are just that tight. Whenever he gets close to the pussy, she creams on herself. As soon as the tip of his tongue brushes across her inviting clit, she loses her mutha fuckin mind. The thing is he goes straight for the gusto, unlike most guys. He actually plays around the clit because he knows clitoral stimulation is the key to pleasing his woman.

Antonio never has to go deep sea diving because he knows Mango better than any of the others. The scary thing is how he went in last night, like it is going to be the last time he will ever see her.

He straight ate the pussy inside out until she squirmed, crawled, pleaded and cried out for him to stop. But, she really didn't want him to stop and that shit turns him on more while he licks the pussy all over without missing a damn spot.

First, his tongue pushes the hood back and makes her toes curl. Then, he slurps on the clit slow and consistently like a baby sucking a mother's nipples. *Oh my goodness*, she can feel herself getting horny, just painting a vivid picture of his craft.

He always tells her how amazing 'Silk' (his name for her pussy) smells and tastes while down there making love to it with his mouth. He likes to have her legs wrap around his neck and locked firmly. He then, grabs her watermelons from the bottom and holds them in the palms of his hands as if he is holding a newborn…gentle, but firm.

Antonio always fulfills her needs and the anticipation makes her shiver whenever he blows on the inside of her wet, but warm thighs. He makes sure he hums, moans, and groans on the pussy to make it wetter or until she grinds 'Silk' back to his lips as if she is grinding on 'Show stopper'.

Even though it takes her some time to cum because most guys be all over the damn place, Antonio brings her in for landing in five minutes or less and leaves her heart beating so hard it feels like it will come out of her chest.

She suddenly realizes her eyes are closed as she hears a familiar song playing from her favorite mixed CD and starts moving and winding her body to the music as Lil' Wayne sings/raps the words to "Wayne Down on Me."

She swears he makes that song for her, so she sings along, starring at herself in her rearview mirror: *"Uhh wide receiver Weezy; throw the pussy at me. The pussy lips smiling...I make the pussy happy. Take them panties off. The pussy looking at me and I'm the pussy monster. Now get the pussy ready. I like to kiss. She likes to kiss. I deep stroke, and make her bite her fist."*

Damn, these lines are making her moist as she relates to the fist biting part. Oh how she dreams of fucking and when it's with someone she cares about, she can really let all that freakiness go and enjoy. Antonio is the one and she knows it, but she will never sacrifice her beliefs to be with any man...not even him. Wayne keeps singing and Lenese's mind starts drifting in a whole different direction:

> *"First class pussy*
> *Crystal glass pussy*
> *I... I get it wetter than bass pussy"*

Damn, the more she thinks about this song, the more she thinks about Janard. Antonio will always be her soul mate, but she needs something more stable and consistent. She needs Janard and she really doesn't even know how she will face Enga today.

Lenese thought about cancelling the appointment and cutting all ties with the Tremells', but her curiosity to find out why Enga cheated is eating at her like a piranha eats at flesh. She is in the mood for more sex after listening to Wayne and really doesn't even have the patience to see this bitch nor listen to her complain about her future man.

Just then, Mrs. Tremell pulls up in her brand new 2012 convertible Jaguar. The damn car is all white, including the interior and plush as hell. It is sitting on chrome 20's, shining like a star. On top of that, she is looking amazing with her hair swept up off her shoulders. This shit just makes her more disgusted with the whole situation.

It has just become clear to Lenese that this 'flight attendant' is using Janard for his money and making empty promises of having a happily ever after. *What a bitch! I know he can't be that blind by love not to see what she is doing.* He deserves so much more and Lenese desires to be the one to give it to him…all of it.

Chapter 11

Back To Business

Dr. Stringfield enters her office to find Enga's section of the file sitting on her desk which means her little fast ass has already checked in and paid. She is still having second thoughts about even working with the Tremmels' because she yearns for Janard in ways that aren't even business savvy. Hell, she doesn't even want to see Enga's face because her "I don't give a fuck attitude," reminds Lenese of her own self, some years ago.

Enga is simply beautiful, flirtatious, and Lenese can tell she doesn't really want to settle down. She uses what she has to get whatever she wants and although Lenese can never be accused of being a playa hater, game recognizes game, and she knows this woman is definitely not a keeper. Lenese has a strong feeling that Enga will talk her head off today and she is thankful for wine and that the sessions are only fifty-five minutes each.

When she picks up the folder and begins to walk over and invite Enga in, she sees a sticky note attached that reads: "***Dr. Stringfield***, Mrs.

Tremmel has a special request of you and I want to give you a heads and thumbs up! LOL," Liz wrote.

Now, what in the hell is Liz talking about? Liz already knows that she is crushing on Janard Tremmel so she better not try to be funny today. Lenese trusts Liz as a friend and assistant. Sometimes, she tells her things that D'Juana doesn't even know and is sure Liz will keep them confidential even though D'Juana is her bestie. That's how rumors leak and Lenese refuses to have her successful business jeopardized because "loose lips sink ships." like her grandma used to say. At any rate, Lenese is more than curious to know what *special* request *Miss Enga* wants to ask of her so she gladly invites her in. Lenese shows her to the lovely couch and offers the traditional glass of Moscato in which Enga gladly accepts.

Before Lenese can get a word out to start the session, Enga begins to speak. "Janard and I are really suffering sexually and although I know our issues are BIGGER than just sex, I have to make sure I want to still be with him. We had a wonderful sex life before he began to hassle me about having kids. Look at this body! You think I want to ruin all of this for a *tax write off?* Things are sooooo good until about a year ago when I switched airline companies and we aren't traveling together anymore. I swear he is so controlling with all this baby talk, and it turns my stomach to think of gaining 50 or more pounds and quitting a job that I love so dearly to sit home and gain more weight caring for a child I don't want." At that moment Lenese doesn't agree with Enga, but she certainly understands. She can't imagine someone being so deceptive and selfish, but she believes this will all backfire on Enga once Janard is gone.

"Janard thinks the world of me and will pretty much do anything to make this marriage work." Enga rambles off. "It is his idea to see a marriage counselor, but it is my idea to see one who specializes in sex therapy because without sex, there is no marriage. So, I did some research and found that you are the best out here and you are sexy as hell!" "Okay?????" Lenese says, lingering on to see what Enga has up her sleeve because of the sexy as hell remark she just made. "So….. (Enga takes a huge breath as if she is about to run a million words down in a little bit of time) we are wondering if you can help heal our sex life by having a ménage trios?"

Lenese can't believe what her ears are hearing. This chic is going to allow her to take her husband that easily? Lenese is sure that she can heal Janard's heart and soul with compassion, understanding, and not to mention the 'wet wet.' Shaking her head to herself, *This can definitely be a win/win situation.* She's always wants to have a threesome, but is a little homophobic.

Lenese wants the experience in case she runs into a couple that is suffering sexually from having one and that way she can lead by example, not to mention how exotic it sounds. Lenese has a slight experience when she was too young to know any better. It was with her childhood best friend and wasn't that bad. She'd kissed a girl (her best friend at the time) and liked it, as Katy Perry will say. And, come to think of it, Enga is just as gorgeous as her and will be the perfect candidate to help complete her own sexual fantasy.

Lenese tells Enga that this is not usually how she runs her practice and that she can refer them to an orgy group that she came in contact with on a business level. She tries to remain professional, but her heart is beating faster and faster as she began to picture Janard's sweaty body pressing up against hers while kissing his lips with a passion and persistence of making him her man.

Enga interrupts her with, "If it's a money issue….," but Lenese stops her dead in her tracks and says, "I have done a lot of things, but a ménage trios has never come up in my history of being a therapist.

What better way can we have "hands on" experience? I will be honored to come into your bedroom and bless you with my expertise." Lenese boasts with confidence.

Lenese opens her mouth to question Enga about how she thinks this will help fix her sexual issues with Janard and why does she want to have a ménage trios with her, but again before she can say a word, Enga starts running it down. "Well, it's every man's fantasy to have a threesome and I just want him to feel comfortable with me again. He hasn't touched me in months, and something has to give. I figure that if we have you there helping us do things we've never imagined, and him getting all the enjoyment he can possibly stand, he will see that withholding sex from me is hurting him just as much and stop this madness. "

Enga's psycho analogy is quite entertaining and somehow true. If she brings the tension away from herself by making this seem like she wants to fulfill his every fantasy, he may actually enjoy it and look at her with new eyes. The only problem is Lenese knows she is the shit in bed and out, so Janard will certainly have new eyes, but they just won't be for his wife. *It must be fate, because this is all happening too easily.* She wondered how she will get Janard to sleep with her, knowing he is deeply in love with Enga and now she doesn't even have to sneak to do it. This has to be too good to be true, but she isn't going to question FATE. No. Lenese is going to take this opportunity to enjoy her fantasy and leave with the man of her dreams.

As they wrap up the session, Lenese gives Enga her personal cell phone number and sets up a follow up appointment to the big event that is going down this upcoming Saturday; only two days from now. She still can't believe that this is actually about to happen, and so soon.

Lenese needs to prepare. She has to hit the mall, get some smell good and sexy ass lingerie from Frederick's of Hollywood. She is going to soak really well tonight to make sure all of Antonio's juices are out of her. She wants this like a fat kid wants cake and she is not going to let anything or anyone stand in the way of her and Janard...her love to be!

Chapter 12

Cruel Intentions

Lenese arrives right on schedule at 9 o'clock a.m., looking around before she rings the doorbell. Her mom always taught her to be aware of her surroundings, especially in her line of work. She is just a tad bit nervous because she doesn't make house calls and she doesn't have many friends that she actually goes to visit from time to time.

The Tremells' live in a nice neighborhood though and she isn't worried by far, looking around is just habit. Lenese is standing there looking fabulous in a black trench coat and stilettos. Underneath, her lingerie is flawless, wearing an all- black Va Bien Satin and Lace Torsolette with matching thong.

She doesn't want to waste time taking off clothes; she will rather get straight to business. Waiting for and wanting the opportunity to put it on Janard, she doesn't have time for small talk or none of that type of dumb shit.

She isn't quite sure how things will turn out with the threesome, but she is going to remain open minded and do whatever feels good to her at the time. The anticipation is killing her and her heart is beating really fast. Her palms are sweaty and her knees seem to be buckling. *What the hell is going on now and why does it feel like I'm about to have sex for the first time?* She is a pro at this type of thing. She really needs to pull that shit together and fast.

Taking a deep breath, she leans forward to ring the doorbell. Janard opens the door wearing a slightly open black bath robe and asks, "Did you find the place alright?" She exhales really loudly and smiles the biggest Colgate smile; gazing at him like a teenager in love. He returns the smile and invites her in, putting his hand on the nape of her ass for guidance.

"Let me take your coat," he suggests in a sexy and seductive voice that makes her weak at the knees. "Make yourself comfortable," he starts to say before taking her coat and seeing that she is already comfortable. He stands there with his mouth wide open, shaking his head, and looking like he can't believe his eyes. Lenese must have really impressed him because he is leaning in towards her like he wants a kiss and whispers, "I'm glad it is you!"

Lenese doesn't even care what the hell he means by that because the scent of his cologne is astounding and her pussy feels like it will burst and flood their beautiful, marble floors. She wants to push him up against the wall and suck the skin off his dick. *Damn, this nigga is fine as shit,* she realizes he is guiding her towards the stairwell.

As she starts walking up the stairs, swears she can feel Janard's breath on the back of her ass but doesn't want to look back and spoil the suspense. It smells like his cologne is filling the essence of their entire home which is fine with her because whatever it is smells amazing. She wants to just stop and get it going right there on the stairs and is ready to act on instinct without even knowing the "threesome" rules.

Janard can sense what she is feeling or can see that entire ass hanging out from that thong, because he steps up behind her real fast, and kisses her on her neck directly behind her ear. *Oh my God, that is my fucking spot. How did he know? Is this my soul mate? Why am I feeling dizzy?* All of these things run through her head as she finds herself on all fours. Her hands are on the step in front of her and her knees are embedded in the crease of second to last step. At first, she thinks she may have tripped and fell or something, but quickly comes to realize that Janard is steering this ship and she can just cruise.

He aggressively pushes her down on the stairs so her back is arched perfectly until it looks like a mountain slope; then he lets the belt loose on his robe. He then grabs a beautiful golden banana-shaped dick that looks like a ray of sun on a rainy day. It hooks to the left and she knows he is going to eat her walls up with that thing. It has to be at least 10 or more inches long filling up his nicely sized, manly hands. It is already hanging freely and Janard wastes no time putting it to use. He then slings it in an upward position and begins to slap her ass with it.

Janard slides it up and down her pussy until it is covered in her juices and continues teasing her while she moans and groans in a desperate way. She is moving her ass in a grinding motion as if she is dry humping the air. Feeling like it is her move; Lenese does the famous "look back" and smiles as Janard quickly drops his 'Mandingo' and starts eating her *'Mango'* from behind.

Janard quickly notices her pussy piercing and begins using it to his advantage. He's grabbing the ring with his teeth just enough to make her jump and squirm and then holds it there while his tongue goes to work. Lenese doesn't expect any of this, but enjoys it nonetheless.

She absolutely adores forceful sex and any movement of that ring is enough to put her out of her reality.

Lenese is totally taken by surprise and damn near chokes on her own saliva. *Is this shit really happening to me right here and right now?* She is so excited that it feels like she has to pee. Her stomach is full of butterflies and her words can't even form to come out of her mouth.

So, she keeps it closed and her legs spread out a little further than they were. Her knees are burning, but then again, so is her head. She feels feverish as if she will pass the fuck out. This man is so on point that Antonio can't even compare. Then again, Antonio has never eaten her this way.

She isn't able to move or go anywhere, especially since he has placed both hands on her ass cheeks and has them spread apart like gynecologist preparing for an annual pap. When she first feels his tongue, it shocks her and makes her pussy muscles clench, but now that he's been licking for at least two or three minutes of which feels like hours to her, she is totally relaxed and feeling so good that she wants to cry from ecstasy.

His tongue is long and thick and feels like it covers her entire pussy with one lick. He doesn't miss an inch of Mango, making long upward strokes starting at the heart of Mango, heading directly for her clit. This is different and stimulates every sense within Lenese's body. She feels tingling from the tip of her toes to her face muscles. *What the fuck is going on here? This shit is feeling too damn good and unlike anything I've ever felt before.*

She thought she'd done it all, but her new boo is teaching her some moves. Oh, he is definitely a keeper and she is ready to tell him, Enga, and the world.

Janard is kissing Mango's lips like they have a face and Lenese is now grinding that ass back in slow, slithering motions of a snake until he sticks his tongue gently inside of her pussy. She thought to herself, *I swear Imma faint right here on these damn steps. He can't just stay in there and eat until all is gone.* Right then, he pulls the tongue in and out like a fucking motion which really makes Lenese breathe funny and feel like she needs an asthma inhaler; sucking up air as if taking her last breath.

Just when she thinks she is in heaven and life can't feel any better than right at that moment, he licks a little further up and swipes his tongue up the crack of her ass. Her knees buckle for real this time and she automatically tries clenching her ass cheeks together because it is her first instinct. Of course she wants this from him, she wants it all, *but damn, can a sister get a break in between?* He then slides it back down and then starts circling his magnificent tongue around her asshole until she feels it get wet like a pussy from the inside.

Goddamn, this nigga is going to have me crazy as hell, is all that clouds her mind, but this time actual words are able to leave her mouth as she screams, "Oh my fucking God, yesssssssssssss!" Janard doesn't let up at all. In fact, he goes for the treat and sticks his tongue inside her asshole, which makes Lenese fucking lose it and stretch her entire body straight out as if someone is playing tug of war with it. She can't move, let alone feel her legs, as she realizes she just came out her ass.

Janard slides his strong, manly arms under Lenese's stomach and rolls her up into his arms like a tootsie roll while her body has no resistance resembling a limp noodle. She is "done done done" as D'Juana will say in her Nicki Minaj voice. Lenese feels as though she has blacked out for a moment and is just being rescued by her Knight in Shining Armor, until she looks around and realizes where she is and what is about to go down. In the back of her mind, she is not up for this with Enga. In fact, she wants to do bodily harm to her at this point.

On the other hand, Janard fucked her so well, that if someone comes to her and says Antonio anything, she will be like, "Antonio. Who is Antonio?" She'd never experienced such forcefulness and compassion all in one sex sitting. He is "the one!" She is certain of that. The way she melts in his arms, gazes into his eyes, stiffens at his touch, lusts for his body, and adores his scent…she is completely sure he is the total package and she can't understand what the hell is wrong with Miss Malibu Barbie.

Because Lenese is a professional and can usually handle any and everything she runs across sexually, she is more than ready to show this bitch what her husband is lacking at home. All of these thoughts are running through her head as Janard carries her to the top of the staircase and hangs a right to enter what looks like a palace. As he opens the door to the master suite, he looks down into her eyes and smiles a smile so big, that she swears she can read his mind. She is hoping that he is thinking what she is thinking; that he is going to devour her all over this small castle.

That is until she sees Enga sitting in the hot tub looking like a super model with her beautiful blonde locks pinned up to make her neck look extra-long and sexy as hell. What is this? Is she complimenting the wench who lives with her future man? She can't help it though. Enga is just that gorgeous and Lenese has to admit that if she was bisexual, she will be chasing her for herself. The bubbles covered her breasts, but Lenese is curious to see if she has any visible body markings or scars. She is very competitive and thinks that her own body is like a Picasso; beautiful to look at, but cherished like an antique.

Janard heads toward the Jacuzzi hot tub as Enga grins, showing all 32 of her pearly whites. He gently places Lenese into the hot tub alongside Miss

Teen USA and tells them to play nice. Lenese thinks it is cute, considering he doesn't know that she really doesn't want to. Before Janard can turn his back to walk away good, Enga eases her way over to Lenese and is on her knees directly in front of her.

Enga reaches her arms out as if inviting a hug from a long lost friend and places them on the doctor's shoulders in a soft and caressing way. Her fingertips are softer than a cotton swab and feels like beads sliding backwards toward her neck and back as Enga fondles her shoulders like piano keys…feeling one finger at a time lover and over again.

Enga then leans in for the kiss and although Lenese is not feeling this shit at all the mood is so wonderful and relaxing that she can't help but let herself go. Hell, Janard just ate her guts out and she doesn't even have the energy to fight her. Besides, this is all about pleasing her man and she doesn't want to seem like a fake in not practicing what she preaches about being open to new things sexually.

In the back of her mind, she is thinking that she really needs a drink some kind of awful as she sees Enga leaning in closer to kiss her with her perfectly shaped and glossed lips. As she feels the softness of Enga's lips, she closes her eyes and imagines she is being kissed by Janard instead. Enga's tongue wraps around hers like a python and slithers all over the place as if it is a frantic child lost and confused. Lenese can smell Enga's hair, perfume, and breath all at one time. The mixture of the three smells like a Baskin Robins with all those flavors bouncing off her body.

She can't believe how well Enga uses her tongue and can't help but to return the favor. So, she grabs the back of Enga's neck and kisses the shit out of her. Both Enga and Janard look shocked as she comes up for air, but Lenese is in the mood now and nothing is sacred any longer. She starts kissing Enga behind her ears, up and down her neck, while taking in small, but extensive breaths of her perfume, which is actually turning her on more.

Then Enga snatches her by the back of her hair and yanks her neck back so she can mock her previous actions. As her lips and tongue move down to the middle of her breasts, she opens her eyes to see Janard standing directly over them both. *Now, that's what I'm talking about,* Lenese's head is already laid back on the top of the tub, so she gives Janard a look that says, "I'm going to swallow you alive." He is very good at mind- reading because he leans down and kisses her passionately making her feel as if she is dreaming. He is actually kissing her upside down, but she doesn't care the least bit.

He licks from her bottom lip to her chin, then down to her neck and she is raging with excitement because by that time Enga has her breasts in her mouth as well. Oh what a feeling this is and she wouldn't change a thing. Lenese takes her arms out of the perfectly warm water and grabs 'Mandingo' at the shaft, pulling and guiding him to the tunnel that is dark, wet, and open for business. Her mouth is literally watering as she imagines his dick will taste like butterscotch.

As she slides his manhood into her mouth with her head hanging back, she feels every inch of it gliding down her throat. She can't close her lips on it just yet because she wants to lick it like a lollipop first. So, she licks it up and down from the shaft to the head and back down again in a slow, but steady motion. Making sure not to catch him with her teeth, she starts licking around the dick in a circular motion; very seductively with her eyes wide open.

Moaning and groaning and handling it with tender, loving care, she makes sure to use her hands as little as possible. Lenese then licks up from the tip of the head to the shaft and keeps going for the nut sack. She feels Janard twitching a little as he realizes what she is about to do. Yet, he is steadily sucking on the other breasts that Enga left looking so sad and lonely.

For a few seconds, Lenese plays and licks all over and around his sack of jewels, but as she feels a hand slide down her stomach and land right on Mango's clit, she slurps them balls right into her mouth full speed ahead. Janard jumps with astonishment at how she does that with no hands. She begins to moan and hummmmmm on nuts because this usually feels like something vibrating and takes her man out of commission.

She is tossing those balls around in her mouth with her tongue like a circus clown and she can tell she has him with the humming because his knees keeps bending in a falling motion. *Ok, it's time to give his ass the business. I'm not even going to be able to do this shit as usual, so I'm going to go straight for the choking syndrome seeing as how I don't have a choice.*

She comes up off the nuts ever so gently and licks back up the shaft, being sure to focus on that vessel that goes down the back of his dick. She licks it softly up and down a few times and moves her way up to the head to engulf it with one scoop. As she plays around with the head, moving her tongue all over and around it, he starts pushing himself deeper into her mouth.

Her lips are welcoming his presence by parting just enough to slide in a little at a time. By now, Janard is standing straight up and has pulled Lenese on the deck of the tub so her entire body lay flat as he is careful not to mess up the works of her tongue while he is still in her mouth. The funny thing is Enga isn't missing a beat, crawling out of the tub right behind her, pushing her leg up at the ankle while kissing and licking her inner thighs.

Although Lenese is very much distracted by Enga's tongue and lips getting closer and closer to 'Mango', she doesn't forget the prize in her mouth and works her jaw muscles as if she is dangling from a cliff and her life depends on it. She grabs his dick with her tongue wrapping around it and using it to pull him further into her mouth while her lips are slipping and sliding from all the saliva until his dick is lying in the back of her throat. Without a second thought, he then thrust his dick in and out of her throat like he is stroking a pussy; bending his knees so he can get it all in.

She notices her airway passage is being blocked now, so that is her cue to take him down and choke on the dick. To her surprise, he pushes further into her mouth and she is really gagging, and damn near coughing which feels delicious to him because the next thing she knows, he is gripping her waist and pelvic area to steady himself. He is cuming and it is awfully hard because she can feel lumps of semen being released from his dick while his pubic area is smooshing her nose in.

Meanwhile, back at the ranch, Enga is licking, slurping, sucking and eating the hell out of 'Mango' like some sort of porn star.

This chick has definitely eaten pussy before and deserves a trophy for doing it better than most men. Enga knows exactly where to go and how long to be there. Right then Lenese feels pleased to be brought to her climax so quickly and unexpectedly, that she squirts all over Enga's face. Janard and Enga look at each other and burst out laughing like they are a wrestling tag team, while Lenese lay there exhausted, and completely out of breath.

Penetration

Now that the ice has been broken and thawed, Lenese is ready to show these two why she is the best sex therapist in Atlanta without hesitation. She is much more relaxed and doesn't feel any sexual tension or harsh feelings towards Enga anymore. In fact, she wonders if Enga is bisexual because she licked her pussy so well that she forgot it was a chick down there.

For the first time she hears music and wonders if it has been playing all along until she notices Janard over by the stereo flipping through CDs. Before she knows it, she hears Plies telling her to "Please Excuse His Hands," and she knows it is about to be on. Plies always put her in the mood to do the damn thing and do it well.

She imagines herself winding her body like an exotic dancer, bending over while touching her toes, and flipping her hair in circles. She is a wild beast that needs some taming and Janard is just the man to do it. As Enga gets out of the Jacuzzi (without a mark on her body, by the way), Janard pulls Lenese up off her back and on to her feet. He has this look in his eyes that makes her feel all warm and tingly inside. Just then, she feels his warm, cotton-like lips pressing against her own and it literally takes her breath away.

This man is draining every ounce of life out of her body when his tongue touches and intertwines with hers. She feels hot mentally and physically. She's never been so turned on by any man other than Antonio, but this time something is different. Although she knows this is not love, she wants Janard for herself, and knows it is going to take more than sex to make him respect and love her. So for now, she is just living in the moment and wishes that she can have that moment for life.

Janard is ever so gentle and loving and he doesn't seem to have a hateful bone in his body. He slow grinds on Lenese for a while; holding her ever so close. Then he starts seductively dancing on her like they are at the senior prom. With lips still locked, like two teenagers in love, he begins to rub all over her body in a sensual manner. Lenese doesn't know where Enga is or what she is doing and frankly she doesn't give a damn.

Janard starts walking forward and backing Lenese up towards the king sized bed which is the moment she has been waiting for. Once they are at the edge, he tucks his strong but soft hands under her ass cheeks and scoops her up until her legs fall around his waist. *Damn that is nice.* She holds on to his neck because she thinks he is about to lay her down on the bed.

Instead, he turns around and sits down on the bed with her straddling him. Lenese grins a quick grin and looks at him with tantalizing eyes. Little does he know that riding is her specialty because she can control, tease, and make love to the dick just like she wants, without any distractions. Janard lifts her slightly and brings forward 'Mandingo' to insert inside of 'Mango'. It takes a minute to work him all the way in so he makes sure to kiss her the entire time. But once he is all the way in, she wants to scream to the top of the Empire State building.

She is cuming already and he didn't even move a muscle or attempt to stroke it yet. "Now this is what I'm talking about, she manages to spill out as she works her pussy muscles as much as she possibly can. Lenese wants him to feel them opening and closing up around his perfectly shaped dick. She knows he admires the workout because he humps her back, while grabbing her ass very firmly, as if he wants to control the entering and exiting of 'Mandingo'.

Of course, this is out of his hands and control, because Lenese begins to rise up slowly while squeezing his dick with her muscles and sliding down on the dick while allowing her pussy to open up, almost feeling like she is going to push the dick out of her. She can tell he isn't used to this because he is staring her dead in the eyes and thrusting her ass towards him in a rowing position.

Lenese knows he is ready to cum because the only time guys change up a position is when it's good to them. Before she has another thought, Janard flips her ass over on her back while trying his best to hold back, and lays her down on the bed with his dick still attached. Boy is he stroking the shit out of the pussy, like a guitar playing the song of her dreams and Janard owns all rights and royalties.

Lenese is seeing double, but taking the dick like a champ. The intensity of it all is amazing and before she knows it, her juices burst from 'Mango' like a tidal wave. Although she thinks she may have blacked out for some minutes, she never stops grinding her throbbing pussy bones up against Janard's nicely shaped pelvic area.

By now, her hair is sweaty and sticking to her face, but she manages to get her sexy on by swishing it from left to right as if saying, "No, no more." The funny thing is, that's how she feels, but it's not what she wants. Instead she raises her ass up off the bed, inviting him to go deeper and make the pussy numb.

He follows body language well because right then he goes under and comes up into the pussy like a pipe exploding from wear and tear.

He is about to bring her to climax again which is unbelievable for Lenese because this is a first. No man ever makes her cum three times during the same sexual session. "Umm, you're amazing Janard," she whispers loud enough to here herself talking, but not loud enough for her lover to hear. That is against the code. Never say his name. Refer to him as baby, love, daddy, papi, etc.

Feeling unsure about him hearing her, she looks in his face for a sign as he leans down on top of her and whispers again in her ear, "I'm glad it is you!" *What does he mean by that? Is it appropriate for me to ask him that while he is making love to me? Do I really believe this? Is he making love to me? He is showing all the signs of making love: kissing me in the mouth, laying face to face with me, whispering in my ear, grinding instead of pounding, and last but not least, the amazing eye contact."*

By then, Enga is standing there with some Hershey's chocolate syrup and whip cream to bring the party alive. The couple looks up with stupid ass grins as if they were busted by their parents or better yet, by their spouses! Well at least they are right about that because Enga's smile quickly turns upside down, but Lenese sees disappointment in her eyes, and wonders why. Although, she isn't sure if it is for Janard or herself, Lenese stares back as Enga's eyes are piercing through Lenese like a dagger in the heart.

Enga quickly snaps out of it because she is trained to go and suddenly smiles with a look of "ok then," holding up the chocolate syrup and says, "Qui veut gouter mon chocolat?" (Who wants to taste my chocolate?) Enga loves speaking French during sex because it makes her feel sexy and desirable. French is the language of love and she sure has it for Lenese. Enga has been trying to get next to her ever since she first read about her. When she saw her photo, she swore she fell in love at first sight.

Enga has always liked women and it is no secret to her husband. He knows of her secret attraction because she confessed it right after he caught her with another flight attendant when they first started dating. The funny thing is it turned him on when she wasn't his property. Once she crossed the "line of war" or as the ole folks will say "jumped the broom" with him, it isn't so sexy anymore.

They had never discussed if Enga will keep her growing fantasy of being with other women and being able to act on them, so Enga figured it was ok. Janard is a good man, but she is young and thinks she can have her cake and eat it too. I mean damn, Enga thought ton herself, It isn't like she is banging another dude!

She was actually surprised when he agreed to the threesome, although she'd lied and told him the doctor suggested this. Janard would have never allowed her to be with another woman after the latest incident. Enga had been sleeping with Janard's best friend, Desiree for about three months before Janard found out. He was devastated that Desiree kept it from him, but expected it from Enga because she is young and wild; just not with his grammar school best friend.

Enga snaps back into the moment when she hears Janard say, "J'aimerais gouter votre chocolat suisse manquer" (I would love to taste your chocolate Swiss miss), falling right in with Enga and the exotic language of choice. Lenese isn't ignorant to what is going on; in fact she speaks fluent French. She took it in college for 3 years and practices on her annual getaways.

"Verser chocolat sur moi suisses manquer et voir comment je peux vraiment douce soit." (Pour your chocolate all over me Swiss miss and see how sweet I can truly be.) Enga must have taken the time to heat the chocolate up because it is very warm, and silky smooth as it falls all over Lenese's breasts, neck, and drips down to her pierced naval, settling in between her pussy lips. Then Enga pours chocolate on her own puckered lips, allowing it to drip down her chin as she kisses her husband's lips, pushing him back away from Lenese until he is in an upright position.

She then puts her leg across Lenese and straddles her facing forward so she can lick the chocolate off of her stomach and titties. This damn girl knows how to use her tongue and with each wet lick, her pussy gets wetter and wetter and Janard is enjoying the chain reaction because the strokes got more forceful as he holds his wife's perfect waist and stares down her ass crack for a double turn on.

Lenese can't work her pussy muscles right because Enga is on top of her so she thinks, *Fuck it, let me enjoy this shit and stop trying to control everything.* Enga is face to face with her again, but something in her eyes is different and Lenese isn't sure if she even wants to know. Lenese closes her eyes and clears her mind of all thoughts while Janard gives her the business and this sexy bitch is about to kiss her.

Enga leans in sideways this time for the kiss. She doesn't want to peck seductively and suck up each other's air just for fun, she wants to make love with her mouth and Lenese can feel it in her bones. She sticks her tongue down Lenese's throat and feels her tonsils, as she is so deep into the kiss. Lenese doesn't mind either, because it actually feels good. Maybe it is her, but women kiss a lot better than men...at least this one does.

Enga starts grinding on her as if she has a dick and Janard is even more aroused. He licks his forefinger and slowly inserts it into Enga's ass without missing a stroke inside of Lenese. Enga comes up for air and seductively says, "Je vous desirez, vous sexy bitch!"(I want you, you sexy bitch) Lenese hears her, but remains quiet while she processes what is meant by what she just heard. *I fuckin' knew it!*

Play along or spoil the moment, is all that clouds her mind when she hears Janard say, "Docteur Merde, votre chatte est tellement humide et merveilleux." (Damn doctor, your pussy is so wet and wonderful). Lenese can't help but to smile on the inside because she feels her man is going to cum harder than he ever did with Enga while she is kissing and licking on her neck, moaning and groaning because her asshole is feeling so damn good.

Flipping her hair from left to right, trying to swallow every bit of chocolate she'd slurped off of Lenese's erotic body. Lenese grinds back to Enga and Janard which must have driven Enga nuts because she does a "Lynn spin" and turns her body around with one instance until she's facing Janard and her ass is sitting up near Lenese's breasts.

Lenese thinks, *A chick's ass has never been this close to my face before, but it isn't all so bad. "Enga's ass is perfect. It is nicely tanned with no panty lines and both cheeks are round like oranges.* In fact, Lenese doesn't hesitate to grab it with both hands on the outsides so she can associate sight with touch.

Man is her ass soft...almost as soft as mine, and she knows how to work that ass like a stripper. The way she began to dip and arch her back after she feels Lenese's hands on her ass, turns Lenese on and again, Janard benefits from the act of lust. Lenese rises up so her pussy can rub against the "pillow soft ass" as she is griping and feels as if she can't get enough of having her clit trapped between a hard dick and a soft ass without getting any direct attention. Before she knows it, Enga got the telepathic signal and did just that. She scoots back so that her pussy is directly on Lenese's lips and bent over to taste the cum Lenese is releasing all over Janard's dick.

Wow! I am going to eat some pussy or carpet-munch for the first time in all my life. I don't know what to do. Lenese is enjoying the attention she is getting down there as she feels Enga's tongue move swiftly, but gently on her clit and sliding down

Janard's dick with vertical strokes. *Everyone deserves to be satisfied*, hyping herself up for this adventure. She is staring at this chick's asshole and even it looks enticing.

She wondered how Enga will act if she stuck her thumb in her ass and her tongue in her pussy. Acting on impulse is what makes her the woman she is today, so she embodies the idea and brings it to truth as she slowly sticks out her tongue, being careful not to abuse it in any way. Her tongue slightly tickles the clit and the warmth of her breath breezes across Enga's pussy until Enga shivers with excitement.

Janard is definitely watching because he starts moaning loudly and saying "Ce droit merde ici est la milleure baise." (This shit right here is the fucking best). All of a sudden Janard's dick is pulled out of Lenese's pussy with lips alone and sucked up into what looks to be an endless, black pit disguised as Enga's mouth.

Janard sticks two fingers inside of Lenese making sure to keep attachment to her some way, and Enga begins to ride Lenese's face. Lenese isn't usually aroused by a man's fingers in her pussy, but then a finger is also embedded in her ass, and takes all the attention away from her pet peeve. She is actually enjoying the feeling of slobber drip off her man's dick from Enga's lips and Enga's tongue all over the place satisfying her and Janard at the same damn time. *This young girl is a bad bitch and if I didn't have to hate her, I would love her.* Lenese closes her eyes, convincing herself to eat the fuck out of the pussy like she will suck the hell out of a dick.

So, she takes a deep breath and begins this new journey. Enga's pussy smells and tastes like peaches in heavy syrup and makes Lenese wonder how her own pussy taste. That makes it much easier for Lenese because smells either turn her on or off and this is definitely a turn on. Her pussy is as smooth as satin and Lenese is eager to feel it rubbing across her face. Taking long, thick licks very slowly up and down her pussy isn't easy because Enga is fucking her face in a counter clockwise position.

Janard withdraws his dick from Enga's slippery wet lips and jabs it back into Lenese's body as if he is being deprived. Enga licks on and around his balls and as he pulls back from Lenese, she slides her tongue down his dick in the opposite direction so he will continue to feel wetness outside of the pussy. Then as he goes back toward her, Enga licks all around the entrance of 'Mango' until his dick fills it up and even then she will slurp on the clit while Lenese grinds back towards her mouth with Janard planted deep inside her.

Enga is enjoying the passion she is experiencing from her bottom end. Lenese's thumb goes further into her ass every time her ass comes down hard on her face from humping her mouth in hopes of feeling Lenese's tongue slide up inside of her. Enga tries to steal the dick from 'Mango' again, but Lenese is prepared this time and squeezes her pussy muscles as tight as she can so Janard can't pull or be pulled out of her and it works.

When she does this, Enga begins to slurp on her clit with cum dripping from her face all over Janard's dick which is going and coming, and Lenese is sucking on Enga's clit so thoroughly that she stops grinding. Janard then grabs Lenese's ass, pulling it to him closer like he wants to be inside her chest and Lenese's G spot is hit all at the same time. The next thing you know, all three are cuming harder than ever and yelling, screaming, moaning, groaning, and exhaling with pure pleasure and excitement.

Chapter 13

What Janard Wants

Janard closes Lenese's truck door and waves her off with a big smile on his face. He is a gentleman first and foremost and wants to make sure that she gets off okay. She seems to have enjoyed herself as much as he did. Then again, it is her job to keep people together and help them out sexually by all means necessary, right?

As she drives off, he wonders what she is like outside of the office. He wants to know personal things about her like, what is her favorite color or her favorite flowers (in case he wants to send some). He admires the way she carries herself like a grown ass woman and doesn't have time for games or nonsense.

She is about her business and that is very attractive. She is a "triple threat!" She is beautiful, smart, and loving. What more can a man ask for? *Oh, damn. He's never considered the thought that she may have a man. Well of course she does.* He wonders if she feels the passion he has in his kisses, hugs, and eyes whenever he looks at her.

He loves her confidence, style, and positive attitude. The more he thinks about it, he likes everything about this woman that is not his wife. Shaking his head quickly to remove the picture of her adoring face from his mind, he turns around and walks back into the empty feeling of this house that was once a home.

Lenese drained every piece of energy out of his body and he needs to replenish it as soon as possible so he heads to the kitchen to make himself a sandwich. He opens the fridge and almost laughs out loud because it seems like everything in it reminds him of Lenese. From the whip crème to the Grey Poupon mustard; all he can imagine is pouring and licking or eating any and every thing off her amazing body.

He has to admit, for a long period of time, he'd forgotten Enga was even there. He truly loves his wife, but she is immature and selfish and he wishes a thousand times that he had waited on marrying her. It was her idea of course to run off and elope in Vegas one day and his stupid, pussy whipped ass did it like a dummy.

Janard is thirty two years old and Enga is only twenty four. They got married when she was nineteen, which is hardly enough time to have lived her life, but she swore she didn't want anyone else to have him. He wasn't in love either, but he enjoyed her company and most of all her youth of living life. In a way, he knew they were not compatible and the eight year age difference doesn't make it any better. Enga likes to live life one day at a time without a care in the world and Janard is a planner and always has future goals.

He thought his feelings would change the longer they were together, but after she cheated on him, he can't bring himself to love her that way again. Oh, the sex is amazing and the best he'd ever had until he ran across Lenese. She is something special and very mature for her age. The funny thing is he isn't sure if it is destined or if his young bisexual wife has other intentions. She has been reading up on the beautiful Dr. Stringfield long before they moved to Atlanta and almost seemed to be infatuated with her and not just her services.

That is neither here nor there right now because Janard is just happy to have made her acquaintance. Lenese brought things out of him physically, emotionally, and certainly sexually that he never thought a woman could. He is feeling her on some relationship type shit, but doesn't know how to approach her.

He isn't sure if she will shoot him down because she is so professional and although he's just had the best sex of his life with her, he isn't sure how she looks at it.

One thing is for sure, he doesn't want to be with Enga anymore. He is thinking about how he will break it off with Enga and be with Lenese without her thinking he just moves from woman to woman like that.

Janard is very attractive and has a great career, and all he wants is "The American Dream!" He wants a family. Although he knows that Lenese had sex with them to help their marriage and could have done this type of thing before, he doesn't care. He thinks she is wonderful and the perfect picture of what a "Lady" should be. He isn't the judgmental type at all. He doesn't care about her past as long as she is willing to let him be a part of her future without secrets and lies.

It isn't about the sex for Janard, it is about making love. Although it wasn't his intention to make love to another woman in his wife's presence (to say the least), he has to admit it is one of the most exciting times in his life. What he didn't expect was for Lenese to come there looking, smelling, and feeling the way she did. When he walked behind her on the stairs and saw that sexy ass twisting in his face, he had to taste it. And now, he wants to keep on tasting it, kissing it, licking it…hell, he wants to marry it.

On his way back up the stairs, he rehearses to himself over and over again how he will break the news to the lovely Enga. He wonders if the timing is all wrong because they did just finish having a great time with the doctor. He is a forward man and doesn't like to beat around the bush about his feelings or wants and Enga knows that about him. But, this time he wonders if he should just take things slowly and try to feel Lenese out before he sabotages his own marriage.

Hell, it doesn't matter one way or another because he is certain the marriage is over. Honestly, it has been over for months and they are just holding on to the hopes and aspirations at this point. As he approaches the door of the master bedroom, Enga meets him, stopping him dead in his tracks. He seems a little startled, but then again, she is playful and jumps out at him all the time. Even though they just had a fuck fest, he still isn't feeling her lying, sinister ass right now.

Enga backs up once she sees the look in her husband's eyes and thinks to herself, *This is it. I know that look and most importantly, I know this man.* She is hoping Janard has forgiven her for being with someone else, and for not wanting children, but the more she thinks about it, the more ignorant it sounds. *How can you forgive someone for not wanting to have your children?*

She answers her own question, *Either you do or you don't!* She realizes that she can't and won't provide what her husband wants and it is written all over his face. "Spill it," she demands when he doesn't give her any eye contact. "What's wrong honey? Didn't you enjoy yourself? Isn't the doctor wonderful?" she begs for conversation. "You looked like you were really into it and I hope we will be able to move forward from this day on."

Janard lifts his face with puppy dog eyes and pours his heart out, "I love you sweet pea, but we haven't been on the same page in a long time. We want different things. I commend you for going through so much trouble with the counseling and everything to mend our broken home and love life, but I will not compromise my wants any more then I will allow you to compromise yours. I guess what I'm trying to say is…I want a divorce!"

Enga's eyes begin to tear up even though she isn't the least bit surprised. It hurts like hell and she doesn't know what to say or do at that point. Yeah, she fucked up and cheated. And yeah, she doesn't want children (right now), but why does she have to lose everything?

She loves Janard, but what she loves even more is the fact that he knows how to take care of his woman. "So, you just realized it after our threesome huh?" she asks sarcastically. She knows the question is loaded, but she wants to see if the man she thought she knew will be honest and fess up.

"Well, I've known for a while, but didn't want to give up on us. Lenese makes me see and feel how a man should be treated, held, kissed, hugged, and loved by a woman," he says with his chest sticking out as if he is about to drum it like Tarzan or King Kong. "I didn't realize what I have been missing baby and I'm not getting any younger ya know? I will help you out until you can manage on your own, but I'm leaving tonight to go stay at a hotel.

I'm going to contact the realtor tomorrow morning and start looking for a buyer immediately. You can keep everything you already have, but no future allowances. We or shall I say, you can find you a nice cozy condo and I can start planning my future with Lenese. he says, taking a deep breath because he didn't mean to say that last part out loud.

Chapter 14

A Woman Scorned

Enga is surprised, hurt, pissed, upset, scared, and most of all vengeful. She isn't sure if this has been the doctor's plan from the beginning. Enga saw the way she looked into his eyes when he was making love to her as if she wasn't even there. How did this happen? *Lenese is supposed to want me after I turned her out. I am not going to lose the woman I'm in love with and my husband to each other,* screamed in her head.

She knows that the whole threesome idea was a mistake now and she can't even tell Janard it was her idea. Maybe he thought that because Lenese suggested it, she really wants him. *How can he be so dumb?* This woman does this type of stuff for a living. That's the whole reason why they went to her in the first place because Enga read up on her and her techniques long before they moved to ATL.

Janard's best friend (Desiree) even knows a guy that she is currently fucking on the regular (as a client of course) named Maurice. She says that Maurice is in love with Lenese and that her skills are unimaginable. Hell, Enga can attest to that now that she's had her for herself and apparently, her husband can too.

This chick has everybody's nose wide the hell open and she doesn't even have a clue. Now all Enga has to do is find out how she is going to handle this situation. She wants Lenese to be comfortable with her before she makes her move on her. Well, that was before Janard decided he wants her too. *Should I threaten her to leave him alone and risk not being able to have her? Should I pretend everything is okay with Janard and just go to counseling sessions and reveal my true feelings? Or, should I just compete with my own husband for the doctor's love?*

Should I blackmail her with the video I recorded during their ménage trios? That is it! That is how she will control this situation like she's controlled all the others.

Enga has always had Janard and every other person she wants wrapped around her cute little finger and things are not going to change now. Let him leave. She doesn't care. She won't shed a tear. He is not who she wants anyway and it is a win-win situation. She's going to get the girl and the money or no one will have her.

Chapter 15

Man Up

Just as he is about to open the door to leave, Enga comes running down the stairs. He doesn't even realize the door bell is ringing because he is so caught up in his own thoughts and wants. He looks out of the blinds and to his surprise; it is the new love of his life. *Shit. I can't possibly tell her in front of Enga.* Once again, he'd forgotten Enga was even there. He is instantly pissed all over again just because he is about to miss out on his chance to unleash all the emotions on Lenese that she left him feeling.

Janard starts acting like a little bitch all of a sudden. He doesn't know what to do with himself. He wants to open the door, but thinks he will put his foot in his mouth because of all that just happened with Enga. *Do I want Lenese to know right away that Enga and I are breaking up? How will that make her feel? I don't want her to think everything that just happened is all in vein and I damn sure don't want her to think I'm some pussy whipped ass nigga that can't handle some extraordinary pussy. I have to play my cards right and tell her how I feel right here, right now.*

"Who is it?" Enga asks with a distraught look on her face, thinking to herself, *What the fuck is he down here doing that he doesn't hear the damn door*. She stares her husband up and down with pure disgust and the look is more than returned as she flings the door open and **Miss Love Doctor** herself is standing there looking like a bag of sweet cotton candy.

Damn! Why does this bitch have to be so fuckin gorgeous? Even though her marriage is on the rocks and it is the doctor's fault, she can't help but return a big, beautiful smile when she opens the door. "Hey, what's wrong?" Enga asked. Lenese feels so comfortable with her right now that she can tell her anything, but she isn't going to tell her what is *really* on her mind.

Something told her to go back and be honest about all her feelings and intents, but now that she is face to face with Enga, she can't bring herself to say it. Honestly, she was hoping that Janard opened the door to ease the stress level, but he didn't and she has to make up something quick so she doesn't look like an ass. "Oh, I forgot to confirm Janard's appointment for tomorrow while I was here," she blurts out.

Right then Janard appears from behind the door and says, "I'll be there with bells on." *What the fuck? He's still going to go to counseling? For what?* Enga thinks. She won't dare ask in front of Lenese because she doesn't want to look or sound desperate, but she is a little confused. *Is Janard going to tell her how he feels about her at the appointment tomorrow?*

Is he going to keep pretending that they are trying to work things out? Are they going to end up having sex together without her this time? The room is spinning and her thoughts are all over the place. She wants to put his ass on blast, but who will it benefit? In a way, she wants to see the doctor stomp all over his stupid ass heart and feed it to the wolves.

As Lenese says "Okay, see you at 10am sharp," she stands there staring in Janard's eyes a little bit longer than she'd planned on doing. It almost becomes evident that there is something else there….some unexplainable feelings or emotions because he's gazing right back into her eyes for just as long. "Uh, um," clearing her throat, she then says, "See you guys," and walks down the stairs twisting her ass a little harder than usual because she knows Janard is watching.

"Um, um, um" Janard moans, as he watches her leave, shaking his head all at the same time as if he can't believe he just had all that in his arms. *Now that's a real woman*, he thinks when his thoughts are rudely interrupted by a slamming door in his face as he turns around to go back in the house. Hell, he hadn't even realized that he walked all the way out and onto the front porch. He feels like a dog in heat and his nose is wide open for this woman. He doesn't give a fuck that Enga is mad or that she'd slammed the door in his face.

He proceeds back into the house to get his things, but doesn't expect Enga to still be waiting there like a damn statue.

"I'm not in the mood for this with you right now Enga," he grunts while kneeling down to pick up his bags. He never anticipated what would happen next. That is until she jumps on his back, yelling and screaming, "You can't leave me!"

What the hell? He starts turning and twisting in circles, still bent over, trying to be rid of this crazy woman on his back screaming in his damn ear.

"Get the fuck off me Enga." he says as he flips her ass over onto her back. "What the hell is your problem?" he screams at her in disbelief.

"I love you Janard. Yes, I've done things in this relationship to hurt you, but they weren't intentional. I don't know how to be a wife. I'm still young and still learning. I fucked up and I fucked up badly. Please give me a chance to redeem myself baby." she sighs heavily from being out of breath.

"You've got to be kidding me. Ashton Kutcher better jump the fuck out of the closet soon and tell me I'm being punked, before I go off in this motherfucker," he proclaims.

"You don't give a fuck about me for real, Enga. You are young, beautiful, and smart and it won't be hard for you to find another dummy to take care of you...preferably one with a clit or you will cheat on him too," he remarks sarcastically. "You are just afraid of me moving on and actually finding happiness. No, that's not it. You want the doctor for yourself, huh? That's more your cup of tea isn't it? Well, I'll do you a favor and deliver the dick to her so well, she might call out your name." he says with a sly smirk on his face.

"I'm getting the fuck outta here." He mumbles and grabs his keys.

"Oh, but it's okay for you to go to OUR counseling session and pretend like everything is okay with us just so you can get some ass? So, what's your plan; to be all emotional, crying and shit about how wrong I did you to get some sympathy pussy? Oh, no. That's right, you think she loves your controlling ass 'cause she fucked the shit out of you, huh?

Well, I got news for you buddy; she fucks all of her clients and your dumb ass ain't no different!"

she yells to the top of her lungs until her throat is burning.

"You evil, little, jealous bitch! How can you say such things? You don't know a damn thing about her. he roars like a lion.

Enga is pretty pissed at this point. Here is the man she's been married to for five years, calling her out of her name and defending another woman that he knows absolutely nothing about over his own damn wife. *What am I going to do*, is all she can think about. The tears fall freely and she can't deny nor ignore them. She falls to her knees, weeping in a praying position, holding her face in the palms of her hands.

That shit doesn't faze Janard the least bit because his young wife is quite the actress and he is tired of this damn saga. *I want a new movie, with a new cast and script.* He walks out the house, slamming the door behind him and feels a sense of relief like taking a first breath after almost drowning.

His first thought is to jump in his Mercedes and follow Lenese, but that is some stalker shit and he isn't going to play himself like that. Because he is a gentleman, he will definitely win her heart and to start he will do something really special for her. *Until tomorrow my future everything*, he thinks as he settles into the driver seat and pops in his favorite mixed Reggae CD.

Chapter 16

Shit Just Got Real

As Lenese pulls off, she can't help looking in the rear view mirror with an unbelievable grin on her face. She wants so badly to tell Janard how she feels about him with his beautiful self, but now obviously isn't the time. *Patience is a virtue!*

God doesn't ALLOW things to happen by mistake…everything happens for a reason. She knows that something good must come from what just happened. Hell, at this point, she is willing to give up everything for real and true love.

She has had her time and now she just wants the husband, kids, and the house on the hill…; the American Dream.

She does feel that karma may come back on her for fucking him so well and giving him the best of her. Deep down inside, God knows her intentions are all selfish and deceitful. Although, she makes a career of screwing married men, she does it with the best interest of their marriages at heart. She doesn't give a damn about them niggas and never takes what they say and/or did to heart.

Janard is just so different and unlike any of the guys she's ever been with. She can pretty much guarantee that he will not have slept with her if she suggested that it would better their marriage. He is a good one and she isn't going to just let him slip away. She starts to wonder if it is Fate that brought him to her. Hell, Enga said it herself that she had been researching her specifically.

The only thing is now Lenese knows for a fact that Enga wants her for herself and doesn't really give a damn about Janard. So, in her mind, she honestly believes there is no saving this marriage, anyway. Sometimes you never really know a person until it's too late. Lenese feels as though Janard is a victim in his marriage because he honestly and truly loves his wife and wants to make it work. The only problem is that it takes two.

Lenese feels like there is something there between herself and Janard that is worth exploring, but first she needs closure with Antonio. Secondly, she needs to get her business in order and only use her knowledge to help future and current clients with their sexual and marital issues. She knows the second thing is going to be a piece of cake, but the first one will certainly be easier said than done.

She's loved Antonio ever since she can remember loving anyone in that way. He is her best friend when she was seventeen he helped her get through a lot of things that changed her life. He was there for her when her mom was on drugs, when her dad died, when she is raped by an ex-boyfriend, and through the so called miscarriage of their child. Yeah, she has had a hard life, but like the Phoenix she rose again. Her problem is, how can she just cut off all ties with this man who has been her rock for damn near her entire life as she knew it?

She knows that they will never be able to stay friends if she gives her all to another. He will always hold her back from truly loving someone else because he holds her heart in his hands. For the first time in her adult life, she is feeling like she can start all over with a clean slate and truly be happy without the "Antonio baggage" that always weighed her down.

It's been only five years since the *baby* situation and she is ready to suck it up and finally tell Antonio the truth. The guilt has been eating at her for all these years and that's mostly the reason why he has this hold on her. She is ready to tell him about the abortion!

Right as she is thinking how, when, and where she can do all of this without fearing for her life, her cell phone rings. It is Antonio. *Speaking of the devil!*

She has been ignoring his calls ever since the night he came over because he always does shit like that. He will show up after months and think they can just fall right back to where they left off. Oh, he will always call, text, email, or manage to keep in touch with her between visits, but that isn't enough for her anymore.

She's told him time and time again that what they are doing isn't healthy for either of them, but he believes they are soul mates and time will work everything out between them. Well, Lenese knows different because she has been hiding this secret from this man for so long. He will hate her and never want to speak to her again. If she would have told him long ago, she would have feared for her life because he is just that crazy over her and has a past that can scare the Grim Reaper.

Lenese is ready though. Knowing that she will have to plan this event just right, she calls D'Juana to get her advice, because they both are the same person, only different ages. She feels like D'Juana is the other twin in her Gemini symbol and she is hers. They are always in sync and besides the baby daddy drama, (which is exactly what Lenese wants to avoid with Antonio), D'Juana is very mature and intelligent for her age.

She is, in fact, the only one who knows the truth about the abortion and swore she would take it to her grave. Lenese just isn't sure if she'd told Liz because they share everything. That isn't her concern right now. She just really wants to hear her sister's voice and see her smiling face because just like a mirror, D'Juana's beautiful personality and attitude will reflect on her.

Just as she turns the corner to pull up in her driveway, God answers her prayers. D'Juana's ass is in her parking space as usual; sitting on the stoop, yapping on her cell phone. She jumps up and hauls ass in the house before Lenese has a chance to yell at her about parking there; looking back grinning like a Cheshire cat.

Immediately Lenese feels like a kid again. She immediately snatches her heels off, throws the car in park, jumps out of the truck, and runs behind her sister as if playing a game of hide and seek. Just the thought of seeing her sister running through the house screaming "Cecily's gonna kill me," (a scene from one of their favorite movies – Eve's Bayou) put a much needed smile on her face and in her heart.

Chapter 17

Just What The Doctor Ordered

After playing the game of cat and mouse with D'Juana, the sisters finally sat down on the floor of the living room on this beautiful bear- skinned rug Lenese got from her visit to Peru a few years back.

"Where you been today Miss Missy?" D'Juana asks, looking at her big sister as if she can feel she is up to no good. Lenese hasn't told D'Juana about the whole Janard situation so this is going to be very interesting to finally have time to run it all down to her "mini-me. "

"We gonna need bottles for this." Lenese replies with a devilish smirk on her face. There is nothing that she enjoys more than talking to her best friend and seeing the look in her eyes and on her face whenever she has a bombshell to drop. She is always ready to hear the latest gossip and although there is the whole "doctor - patient confidentiality" thing with her job, she tells D'Juana about all the dudes she is sleeping with and why.

Once Lenese is done telling D'Juana everything down to the Ménage, she sits there and waits patiently for her response, but her little sister is speechless. She looks to be in shock and that scares Lenese.

"Damn chick, what is your problem?" Lenese asks. As soon as the words leave her lips, that wonderful smile that melts ice comes across D'Juana's face as she leans in closer to her sister and says,

"BITCH! This ain't nearly enough alcohol to consume all the shit you just told me and we need to take this to the bar."

Hell, I need a few shots and beers and I don't even drink brewskie!" D'Juana smiles while shaking her head in disbelief at her older sister. "I love the way you stay true to your Geminism bitch. Damn, I want to be just like you when I grow up pimpin, pimpin, pimpinnnnn!"

"Cool with me twin, but we taking the Beamer tonight, chica! Bow! That's just what the doctor ordered too. Just let me shower and shave and slip on something comfy. Oh, and it's just us tonight.....sorry Liz!" Lenese demands with sympathy for Liz.

The ride to Kelly's Bar and Tavern isn't awkward at all because Lenese knows that her sister never judges her. In fact, they bump Jeezy all the way there, dancing and singing to the top of their lungs with the windows and top down. Lenese is anxious to hear what her better half has to say about this whole mess, but she also knows that once she gets liquored up, she is going to cuss her ass out for keeping it all from her so long. D'Juana is a character when she has a lot of alcohol in her system. Hell, the last time they ended up dancing on the bar at the club and damn near stripping.

Lenese loves it though and wouldn't change her for the world. She is young and she keeps Lenese looking and feeling young too. Their times together can and will make any other friends jealous and they often deal with a lot of stares and snarls from chicks around the area. They are the 'bopsie twins', so they don't give a damn about what anyone else thinks of them. D'Juana will always burst out singing "Don't hate me cuz I'm beautiful," in her best Keri Hilson voice whenever they enter any spot.

Tonight isn't any different except for the fact that they aren't dressed to impress as they usually are. That doesn't mean a damn thing because all heads turn as the Gemini sisters walk through the doors and seats become available at the bar with a quickness. They look at each other and giggle as they both bask in the attention.

Lenese sees a group of sexy ass dudes that look to be between the ages of 23 and 30. They all get up off of their stools and point to the seats to alert the sisters of the vacancies. Lenese winks at the sexiest one to make sure he knows she is interested or at least she appears to be. This is usually the act that gets them free drinks all night long and they both play their roles pretty damn well. As the sisters get closer to the end of the bar, they have a clear view of the pool tables and karaoke section.

D'Juana yells out, "Get yo ass up there and sing the damn song Anna Mae!" Lenese looks at her baby sister and rolls her eyes because D'Juana already knows that she needs to be liquored up before she gets on the mic. Singing is her private passion, but she isn't as eager or willing to sing without some alcohol in her system.

"Get yo ass up on the bar and do that Coyote Ugly shit you do!" Lenese yells back at her, still rolling her eyes, but smiling at the same time. D'Juana puts one foot on the stool as if she is about to climb up on the bar and Lenese smirks at D'Juana and says, "I'm not messing with yo crazy ass tonight chic!" and takes a seat.

"Hello, we have business here tonight, remember?" Lenese asks quietly.

"Oh, ok that's right. Imma be good…..well, Imma try!" D'Juana reassures her.

Just as Lenese is about to thank the handsome gentlemen for giving up his seat, she notices someone out of the corner of her eye and quickly turns her head to see if her mind is playing tricks on her. *Oh my God. I know that's not who I think it is.* She quickly turns her head because she isn't sure if she wants to be seen or not right at that particular moment.

D'Juana's ass doesn't miss a beat and quickly calls her twin out on her awkward actions.

"Bitch, what the hell is wrong with you? You acting like you just saw a ghost or something. she remarked sarcastically. "I know who the hell it better not be, up in the piece tonight; Antonio's black ass!" she says smacking her perfectly glossed lips and scanning the area to see who has her sister in such a shock.

"You gonna tell me or what? Damn!" she insists on knowing.

"Alright, alright, alright. Look around slowly and carefully. Who is the finest dude in here? Take your time and look in all the nooks and crannies," Lenese says reluctantly.

"What, is he giving you the eye?" D'Juana asks and nosily insists.

"Just do it, damn!" Lenese as D'Juana's eyes begin to slowly look around the room, she spots this guy that looks like he just stepped out of a GQ magazine.

This nigga is fine as hell and can pretty much guarantee he is the one Lenese is talking about because he is standing out in the crowd like a little white boy in the ghetto.

Turning to Lenese, she nods her head in the guys' direction to see if she is right and gets the nod of approval.

"Ok, what's his story? You know him?" she asks desperately awaiting an answer.

"Yeah, I know him. That's Janard! " she smiles and replies, watching her sister's jaw drop in disbelief.

Lenese is feeling hot and flustered all over. She isn't sure if she wants to go over there and take yet another opportunity that God has presented or try not to be noticed to avoid any awkward conversations. The thing is, she isn't alone and apparently it isn't her decision to make so she sees. D'Juana gets her ass up from all the attention she is

Chapter 18

D'Juana's World

Lenese is still feeling a little nervous about what her other half will come out and say, but then she's sure that D'Juana will never leak anything to hurt her career or love life. Janard actually looks happy to be in Lenese's presence and it is showing all through his body language. When he pulls out her chair, he scoots it a little close to his own as if they are on a date or something.

Lenese doesn't mind a bit because the gesture kind of breaks the awkward feeling of wondering how he is feeling about her. As D'Juana sits on the other side of her sister at the round table, she has this smirk on her face that signifies deceit and Lenese quickly asks her, "What do you want to drink shawty?"

D'Juana blurts out, "Irish trash cans seem to be perfect for tonight. We have the option to get drunk and the energy to do whatever needs to be done afterwards."

Then D'Juana leans in closer with a song, "When I see you;" singing in her best Fantasia voice which actually sounds like a cat crying. Lenese is known as the singer of the family and thought about pursuing a career in music, but learned that helping people with their marriages and sexual manners soothes that emptiness inside of her more than singing does.

At first Lenese is a little upset that she isn't able to tell her sister

all her feelings and deepest fears about what happened between the trio, but thinks that she can actually learn much more by being in his presence and seeing how they mingle and act around one another. Sometimes you just have to let things play themselves out and not over think too much of what is going on at the time.

Mainly, she appreciates the fact that Antonio doesn't cross her mind much whenever she is with Janard. He has always been that thorn in her side whenever she tries to deal with guys outside of her business; always worrying and wondering if he will pop up and claim her like a lost treasure. Although she loves running into him, she can't stand to see him walk away. It is better described as being bitter sweet.

At this point in her life, Lenese knows exactly what she wants. She just doesn't know who she will share these feelings and aspirations with. She doesn't believe in rushing things either, knowing that everything happens for a reason and that God doesn't make mistakes.

She must have had a serious look on her face while in deep thought because before she knows it, Janard's beautiful face is inches from her own and he is saying something to her. It feels like a dream and she doesn't want to wake up. Lenese feels his hot but icy cool/minty breath breathing in her face and she thinks about puckering up her lips for a kiss.

He leans in a little closer and whispers "Are you ok?"

She quickly snaps out of her thoughts and come back to the real world. "Oh, I'm fine. I'm sorry. I just have some things on my mind." She says reluctantly looking at D'Juana who has the um hummm look all over her face.

D'Juana is like the twin that can feel whatever Lenese is feeling and from the look on her face; D'Juana knows she is thinking about Antonio's sorry ass. Oh, D'Juana doesn't dislike Antonio as a person; she dislikes how he always breaks her sister's guard down, only to leave her hanging time after time.

Of course knowing the story, she understands his reasons, but that doesn't heal the hurt and pain that occupies her Lenese's heart at the mere thought of him.

D'Juana is very much in tune with Lenese's feelings, goals, aspirations, expectations, and sense of being. Hell, she knows her better than she knows herself. This is a woman of strength and love and is always in control. Her big sister is about her business first and love comes second.

She is very different from D 'Juana in that way. Maybe it is because D'Juana is younger or because she is having a child and her motherly instinct is kicking in. However you look at it, these two look alike, but are so very different. It is kind of like missing a whole half whenever they don't talk for a while.

D'Juana looks up to her big sister and always makes sure she has her back in whatever situation, but she's never told her sister how disappointed she's been with her after the abortion. This is something that she will take to her grave because she can only imagine how hurt Lenese will be if she thought D'Juana (of all people) was judging her.

Since D'Juana is the only one who knows, she really doesn't have a choice but to keep it to herself. She can't tell her bestie, Liz. Not because Liz works for her sister, but because she is loyal and can keep a secret.

Plus, she will have to tell everything for Liz to even understand and that is way too much information in D'Juana's book. Many of the times she wanted to tell her child's father, Reo, but he is an alcoholic who cheats on, fights and, degrades her in public; acting just like it never happened hours after. He is an alcoholic and not at all trustworthy and will probably tell Lenese just to piss D'Juana off and cause confusion as the miserable usually do.

D'Juana will pay someone to tell her why she ends up with such a person, especially dealing with her dad's alcoholic behavior growing up. She just chalks it up to the old cliché that women look for men that imitate their fathers, whether it is bad or good. Lenese says that women usually search for the characteristics of their fathers, mainly for the security.

There have been numerous occasions when she wanted to keep it one hundred with her idle, but fears her response and can't bring herself to say anything. D'Juana just can't wrap her head around how a person so gentle, so caring, so loving, and so God-fearing would abort her baby.

When they were young, they always talked about having kids and them growing up and playing together. D'Juana just figured that if her sister/best friend/other half that she'd lived with all her life, could kill her own baby to "protect" it and herself from this guy and his way of life, why the hell did she continue to deal with him?

She could never explain why or how her twin dealt with all those emotions and self-hatred until she found out how she is sleeping with her damn clients. She read about women who unattached themselves in a sexual manner…kind of like a man, but she's never experienced it herself. She isn't sure if this characteristic has always been in her sister, but she does understand how it became apparent after all that.

Her sister wants and needs real, true love in her life and she's never seen Lenese as comfortable, happy, or replenished as she's seen her with Janard tonight. *This can all turn out to be a good thing,* she thinks. *Maybe all Karma isn't bad after all,* tuning into the sexy looks and body language between Lenese and Janard.

He is attempting to feed her the drink he ordered for her while she is in her daze. Although D'Juana is just beginning to feel like the dreaded 'third wheel,' she doesn't want to leave her sister there alone. Taking a very small swig of her drink, looking around, she proceeds to grab the guy that is standing closest to her to dance when Reo comes bringing his boney, cheating ass up in there with some skank.

"Oh, ok that's right. Imma be good.....well, Imma try!" D'Juana reassures her.

Just as Lenese is about to thank the handsome gentlemen for giving up his seat, she notices someone out of the corner of her eye and quickly turns her head to see if her mind is playing tricks on her. *Oh my God. I know that's not who I think it is.* She quickly turns her head because she isn't sure if she wants to be seen or not right at that particular moment.

D'Juana's ass doesn't miss a beat and quickly calls her twin out on her awkward actions.

"Bitch, what the hell is wrong with you? You acting like you just saw a ghost or something. she remarked sarcastically. "I know who the hell it better not be, up in the piece tonight; Antonio's black ass!" she says smacking her perfectly glossed lips and scanning the area to see who has her sister in such a shock.

"You gonna tell me or what? Damn!" she insists on knowing.

"Alright, alright, alright. Look around slowly and carefully. Who is the finest dude in here? Take your time and look in all the nooks and crannies," Lenese says reluctantly.

"What, is he giving you the eye?" D'Juana asks and nosily insists.

"Just do it, damn!" Lenese as D'Juana's eyes begin to slowly look around the room, she spots this guy that looks like he just stepped out of a GQ magazine.

This nigga is fine as hell and can pretty much guarantee he is the one Lenese is talking about because he is standing out in the crowd like a little white boy in the ghetto.

Turning to Lenese, she nods her head in the guys' direction to see if she is right and gets the nod of approval.

"Ok, what's his story? You know him?" she asks desperately awaiting an answer.

"Yeah, I know him. That's Janard! " she smiles and replies, watching her sister's jaw drop in disbelief.

Lenese is feeling hot and flustered all over. She isn't sure if she wants to go over there and take yet another opportunity that God has presented or try not to be noticed to avoid any awkward conversations. The thing is, she isn't alone and apparently it isn't her decision to make so she sees. D'Juana gets her ass up from all the attention she is getting and starts walking right over in Janard's direction.

What the fuck is she doing? I'm going to choke the shit out of this chick if she goes over there. Lenese can't get herself or her thoughts together. She has this dude all in her ear trying to buy her a drink and she just wants to vanish into thin air. In fear of looking like a school aged child, she hurries to her feet and damn near runs to catch up with her slick ass twin.

As they both approach the table, she can't do anything but smile when he turns around looking as sleek and debonair as one man can look. She can smell him from almost five feet away and wants to melt when he realizes it is her and smiles that smile that makes her pussy wet. *Damn, this nigga don't know what he does to me*, she thinks with eyes focused and locked in with his.

"Well Damn! I guess you don't need me after all, huh?" D'Juana whispers in her little sarcastic tone.

"Uhhh Janard, this is my little sister, D'Juana." Lenese manages to break away from the gaze to introduce her.

"Nice to meet you. I can certainly see the resemblance. Have a seat," he says getting up to pull out chairs for them both.

"Don't mind if we do." D'Juana accepts with a huge smile on her face.

Chapter 19

Act Like A Lady

D'Juana is stuck. She doesn't like being caught off guard. As a Gemini woman, she usually sees things coming and mentions of it as a "gift" in so many words. Her blood starts boiling and she can feel her arm pits begin to perspire heavily. Hell, she is sweating under her bra, down her neck and back, and the temperature hasn't changed a bit.

It's safe to say that she is hotter than fish grease and ready to react. She forgets about the guy she was about to dance with or does she? She decides that tonight isn't the night to act out over this no good ass nigga and although she wants to tackle his dumb ass, she will much rather have a blast with her big sister, her new found love, and somebody's son up in the joint. She grabs the guy as if she doesn't see Reo's punk ass and heads for the small dance space. Busy from concealing the negative thoughts racing through her mind, she doesn't even notice the song that is playing.

It is 'Holding You Down' by Jazmine Sullivan and that's what he seems to always have her going in…damn circles. She stares him up and down and is really feeling kind of froggy, but she knows in her heart that if she starts something, Lenese won't come back out with her for a long time. Hell, she didn't even get a chance to tell Lenese that she is pregnant with Reo's baby.

In a way, she is in denial about it and doesn't feel like it will really be real until she shares it with her big sister and mom. She is scared that Lenese will break down with happiness for her sister, but remorse for herself. So, D'Juana's original plan was to go to Lenese's house and tell her so they could cry and hold each other all night like they did when they are kids.

They are playing the wrong Jazmine Sullivan song. They should be playing "Bust the Windows Out Your Car, D'Juana thinks, feeling disgusted. She can't take her eyes off this funny looking dude she can't shake from her heart and/or soul. He is about 5'10 and weighs about 100 pounds soak and wet. He isn't a 'G', but he thinks he is. He has no swag and is quite the corny dude.

He is in the military or what Liz calls a 115, which means he gets paid on the 1st and 15th of every month. His dark completion is scarred with bumps that look like he has adult chickenpox and very thick eyebrows. His best asset is his long, curly, full eyelashes which are almost feminine. He doesn't have a bad grade of hair, which he keeps in a low César.

You can tell by the way he dresses that he isn't a "local" dude. He wears his shirt tucked in, with a belt, and skinny jeans that looks like they are falling off or hanging on by a string. He has on a jean jacket that is always too big and he keeps a fresh pair of Jordan's at all times. She really doesn't know what D'Juana sees in this dude because the one she is dancing with is 10 times better looking. All she remembers is D'Juana telling her nigga can put it down in the bedroom like no dude she's ever been with before.

How he introduced her to things that she could never forget and like having a threesome. The only scary thing about that is she is left feigning more for the chick than for Reo. Lenese told her that all females are bi-curious and that most of them follow up on these fantasies. In fact, she wants to share how she really wanted to pursue the other girl and see if she feels the same or was she just feeling the heat of the moment. She's even been involved in an all-girl threesome and it is wonderful...stress free, no drama; very sexual and seductive.

Now that she is pregnant, everything is about to change. She just went to the doctor that morning and hasn't even shared the news with Reo yet. Now she is having second thoughts about telling him at all. His lying, cheating, dirty dick ass makes her sick to her fucking stomach. Then the nasty, skank bitch he is with doesn't make it any better. Oh, D'Juana doesn't know her personally, but just looking at how she walks and what she has on is enough to gather all the evidence of hoochieism that she needs.

She wants to pull each and every one of her micro braids out one by one and mop the floor with her face. Deep down she knows she can't be mad at the woman because she is an innocent party involved, but she wants to trip Reo up so he can fall face first into a pool table and she can plunge an eight ball in the back of his big ass head.

The cutie is saying something to her, but she doesn't hear a word. She barely sees him standing in front of her. Instead she sees red like a bull and it becomes relevant to her that she will not be able to ignore his punk ass any longer. The guy she is dancing with seems like the type whose down for whatever, but her heart is breaking slowly and she doesn't want to bring him into any of her drama.

So, she excuses herself from the dance floor and goes to walk back towards the table where her sister and Janard are sitting, but it is empty. She feels nervous as she scans the pool room looking for a familiar face so she won't wild out up in this piece.

She frantically begins walking toward the bar area when a guy pulls her by her arm so he can speak with her. Although she doesn't mean to, she snatches her arm away and gives him a look of disgust. D'Juana is totally out of character but right at that moment; she isn't sure how to handle her feelings and emotions. She needs her big sister to talk that psycho- babble to her and keep her ass out of jail.

She turns her head back towards the table to see if they may have passed by her some way, shape, or form and locks eyes with Reo. Her heart starts racing as she tries to ignore his stare. He is waiting for her to act a damn fool because he is dancing all over with the skank bitch. Just as his sorry ass cut a slick ass grin and D'Juana heads his way, Lenese and Janard pop up out of nowhere and Lenese grabs her by the waist pretending to do a sexy/seductive dance behind her while winding her body around; going down to the ground.

She then, turns D'Juana around to continue their freak-nasty dance until she notices the look on her face.

"What's wrong beautiful?" Lenese questions with the most concerned look on her face.

"I gotta get the hell outta here," D'Juana replies as tears began to run down her cheek.

"What the hell is wrong with you," Lenese demands as she grabs D'Juana by the shoulders; slightly shaking her.

"Bum ass boyfriend at 10 o'clock," she nods trying to hold it all together.

Lenese is trying to pull her own thoughts together so to offer the best advice she can in this situation, but she had a little more to drink than D'Juana. Hell, come to think of it, she had a lot more to drink than D'Juana and that isn't normal. Lenese already had a drink at the house, and then she drank both drinks Janard purchased for her and her sister. *Wait a damn minute; this chick never passes up on alcohol...especially alcohol she doesn't pay for.*

Lenese's begins to put two and two together. There is nothing slow about her by far, and she quickly remembers that D'Juana didn't even drink at the house before they came out. Oh, she poured a drink, but Lenese saw the glass in the sink when she went in the kitchen to turn the lights off before they left. She also saw the wetness on her stainless steel sink that is perfectly dry before D'Juana got there.

What the fuck is going on here? This chick always has her shit together and this isn't the first time she saw this bum ass dude in public with another bitch either. Any other time, D'Juana would walk right up to the nigga and tell him to kiss her beautiful, black ass or whatever. Then she will snatch up to the next dude in a sexual manner, and proceed out the door or onto the floor. Shit like this never fazed her before, so what is she crying for?

Lenese snaps out of her thoughts when D'Juana yanks loose from her grip and the next thing she knows, D'Juana breaks a bottle over Reo's head and he hits the floor bleeding out of control. The girl played her cards right and got the hell out of dodge while Janard advices Lenese that they should do the same thing. D'Juana is standing there screaming, shaking, crying, and looking damn near insane. Lenese runs over and grabs her by the back of her shirt. As D'Juana almost trips over her own feet, she realizes he is hurt and falls to her knees to console him.

"See, this is some back woods shit right here. Let's fuckin' go before yo ass go to jail tonight," Lenese screams at her sister.

"I can't leave him here like this Nesie," D'Juana cries.

Lenese can tell she is scared because that is the nickname D'Juana gave her one time when they were kids and they saw their dad beating on their mom. She only uses that name when she is scared and Lenese feels helpless. What is she supposed to do?

Janard disappears and Lenese doesn't even notice until he comes back with a towel from the bar to wrap around Reo's head. Lenese is so glad he is there. She feels safe and protected. She's never imagined going through something so personal with him or in his presence rather, the first time mingling outside of work. Reo sits up with D'Juana helping him to get his balance. She is soooo sympathetic and apologetic while he just sits there in a daze looking as though he doesn't know who or what hit him.

Right then, Jacob comes running over to assist and to get them out of there before the police comes. Jacob does security there and he is also a close friend of the girls because they all grew up together.

"Get her and him the fuck outta here….NOW!" he whispers in a strong, stern voice so his manager and/or co-workers doesn't hear his advice.

So, Janard falls right into play, grabs Reo by the arm, and pulls him to his feet while D'Juana holds the towel on his head, nodding to Lenese in the direction of the door. They all walk out of the bar as fast as they can with a wounded man on deck.

Chapter 20

Everyone Has A Past

Once Jacob gets his friends out of the bar and everything seems to have calmed down, he grabs his cell phone and walks out in the lobby area to call his good friend, Antonio. He isn't sure what happened or what will happen next, and he just wants to make sure Lenese and D'Juana are okay and get home safely. He knows Lenese had a few drinks and isn't quite sure if she drove or rode with D'Juana.

He couldn't even follow them outside because he didn't want the police to question him if and when they came. Nevertheless he is concerned and when Antonio commenced to telling him that he'd been trying to call Lenese all night that night and for the last couple of days, Jacob is caught off guard. Antonio always keeps a cool and calm demeanor but right now, he sounds frustrated and a little pissed with the information he is being fed.

"Where are they now," Antonio asks.

"I'm not sure," Jacob replies, further explaining why he didn't follow them outside.

"OK. Thanks man!" Antonio says in a hurry as if he can't get him off the phone fast enough.

It just so happens, Antonio is at the Apple Bee's right down the street watching the game. He decides to go by there first to see if he can catch her and find out what happened and make sure she is okay.

So, Antonio hollers at the bartender, "Kevin I'll be right back," and walked out the door.

All he can do is keep thinking that he needs to talk to his baby and let her know he is ready to settle down. After all, why else won't she return his calls? Lenese always acts like this after one of their rendezvous, but she is taking it to a whole new level this time. His baby is extra sensitive and he never means to hurt her, but the man inside of him has to take care of business at all cost first and foremost.

He can't believe she was at the bar drinking and having a blast, ignoring him like he doesn't mean shit to her. She's been acting really funny lately and he hasn't even spoken with her since he left her house last weekend. He is so deep in thought that he has to take a deep breath to calm down and not make this thing more than what it is.

This is the only woman in the world he's ever loved and it feels like a piece of his heart is being ripped out of his chest every single time she rejects him in any way.

They grew up together and have been best friends for a little over 10 years. He knew the first time he laid eyes on her that she was special and would always be a part of his life. Never in a million years did he know that she will fulfill him inside and out.

He watched this frail little caterpillar blossom into a beautiful butterfly right before his eyes. She was gorgeous, smart, genuine, loving and just everything he'd ever imagined the perfect woman to be.

Yet, he is scared to give in and up on his lifestyle. Hell, it is all he knows.

He didn't go to college and has never just been a regular Tom, Dick or Harry.

He enjoys the finer things in life and loves being able to give this woman everything and anything her heart desires. She doesn't deserve to struggle like she did coming up and this is the only way he knows how to be there for her whenever she wants or needs him to be.

In high school he played football and even got a scholarship to Atlanta A & T where he had scouts from the Dallas Cowboys checking him out. That all ended the night after graduation when he got shot in the back and his cousin, Demetrius, was killed. The bullet is near his spine and they didn't want to risk him being paralyzed if he got hit wrong or anything like that. All his hopes and dreams and everything he'd worked so hard for all his life was over in an instant.

He was young and very smart, but didn't have any other interest in school or learning a trade. All he was good at was selling drugs and demanding respect.

He didn't have any family here to help him out either. His family were all back in New York, where he grew up, then he moved to Atlanta when he is sixteen after his stepdad left them.

He was too much for his mom to handle with 5 other brothers and sisters, especially after his oldest brother had been killed in the streets the summer before. So, he went to Atlanta to live with his cousin, RaSean, and his pregnant girlfriend instead of hanging around to most likely end up in prison. RaSean was only nineteen, but he had his shit together and made a nice home for all three them.

The first order of business was to punish the guys that killed Demetrius and he knew just how to do it. He knew the police weren't going to do a damn thing; hell, they never did. Black on black crime was the New York way of living and forced him into this lifestyle. The cops don't have a clue about the whole thing because (as usual) there weren't any witnesses around. All they knew was fellas met in an old abandoned warehouse that night about five minutes from Demetrius's house.

Not that Antonio's ever trusted the police to do anything about it in the first place; he used them to get some information before he could go through with his plan. He staked out their whereabouts including parents, relatives, girlfriends, etc. He watched carefully for routine and to see how often they visited these people so he could use them as leverage if need be.

Antonio is smart and this craft is a well arrived one. He thought about kidnapping the "innocents" but decided that would bring too much attention. Instead, he would catch them all together or one by one; it really didn't matter to him how he got them as long as he got them...and he did. It took a total of three months to avenge Demetrius, but once he did, he laid his mind to rest. Although it couldn't bring Demetrius back, it brought some closure to the whole tragedy.

Antonio always seemed to have his shit together and not be afraid of anything or anyone, but he was always afraid of Lenese leaving him like everyone else in his life who he gave a damn about. *Lenese thinks she knows the real me, but she doesn't. She only knows the God fearing guy who has this image to keep up in order to keep his money coming without any issues.*

Lenese knows my deepest fears, my most intimate secrets, and she never judged me. She always has me on this pedestal that I never thought I could live up to, nor deserved to. She was sure that I would never take a life unless it was in self-defense, or at least that's what she assumed. I don't know how to tell her what I've done or how I planned it, so I will just keep it to myself.

That night is still fresh in his head as if it just happened and even to this day, he still has nightmares about it. He wants to share the details with Lenese, but she will never ever want to hear such things. Although she is his best friend, he keeps this secret between him and God. He has some deep rooted anger issues that came from his step father beating on his mother when he is younger, and thinks hurting people is the only real way to get through to them.

He always sits back and pictures himself killing his stepfather and burying his body over and over again, but this is a side of him that he will never reveal to the love of his life. She thinks that his stepfather left them when he is fifteen and was never heard of again, but she doesn't know or would have ever thought that Antonio had anything to do with his disappearance. The family chalked it up to him just leaving Antonio, his mom, and other siblings for another woman and kept it moving.

Antonio *knows*. He remembers the precise spot where he buried him after he watched him take his last breath at the mercy of his own hands. He isn't a coward and he never used a gun to do it; he strangled him and watched his eyes lose life and never said a single word to him during the assassination.

With each memory, he feels justice has been served and realized, at a very young age, that most of his problems in his life may have to end this way.

He has always been very jealous over Lenese and that scares him more than anything he's ever gone up against. This woman should and someday will be the mother of his children and he can't even imagine her living happily ever after with some other dude. He was just too damn stubborn to let go of the street life while the getting is good to settle down and make babies. But, now he is ready.

He loves this woman with every ounce of manhood he has within and can't put her through all the heart ache, pain, and worry as he's done in the past. In fact, that's what he's been trying to call to tell her, but she won't return his calls. Lenese has never gone this long without calling him back and he is a little more concerned than anything else. He's always trusted her with any and everything and doesn't for a moment think she has possibly found someone else.

Am I delusional? She is a sexy ass woman that any man will want on his arm and in his life.

What if she has found someone else and doesn't know how to tell me. What if she is with the guy right now? What if she's having sex with someone else? Ugh,. he tries to clear it out of his mind because it is beginning to drive him crazy. All of a sudden his concern turns into rage as the thought of Lenese with another man starts running around in his head like little Indians around a camp fire. It does make sense though.

She'd never ignored his calls before, even when she cursed his ass out, threw things at him, or even claimed to hate him; she couldn't go an entire 24 hours without calling him back. He is worrying again, but not for her safety this time. Obviously she is fine if she is lolli- gagging at the bar. "She's probably meeting the nigga up there or something," Antonio thinks out loud. "I hope I can catch her ass with somebody!"

He presses down harder on the accelerator as his rage begins to get the best of him. He can see the

"Kelly's" sign right ahead and he can't get there fast enough. His heart is going a mile a minute and he doesn't even notice how heavy he is breathing. He has that look in his eyes and is preparing himself for what he might see. His palms are sweaty but that doesn't stop him from gripping the steering wheel tighter until his fingers are aching.

Blocking out the music playing, he feels like one of those cartoon characters with smoke blowing from his ears and the top of his head. He is so far "in the zone" that he doesn't hear all the horns blowing at him as he hits the accelerator faster to make the light that has already turned red. Out of nowhere, a Yukon Denali XL comes and smashes into Antonio's Dodge Charger on the driver's side and pushes him down the street about a tenth of a mile until he is able to stop.

Even then, the Charger is still sliding sideways down the busy intersection at about 20 miles an hour until it slams into a power pole. The car is smoking very badly and all you can see are people yelling, screaming, pointing, and running towards the car to try to help him get out. A guy almost crashes as he jumps out of his nearly moving vehicle to give aid to Antonio. Just as he is about 10 feet away and still in motion, Antonio's car blows up and burst into flames.

Chapter 21

The Long Ride Home

As they walk to D'Juana's car to place Reo in the front seat, Lenese realizes that D'Juana will need to take him to the hospital. Personally, she is in no frame of mind to go there tonight. Not to mention the fact that she feels he deserved what he got and doesn't care for him anyway. *Karma is truly a bitch.*

She turns and looks at Janard in a desperate manner and asks him if he can give her a lift home. Janard places his hand on the small of her back, smiles and says, "Of course I will take you home. You sure you don't want to follow them to the hospital?"

Lenese is a little irritated because she definitely doesn't want to go to the hospital, but doesn't want to seem non sympathetic to her sister's needs either. But, she can't be fake about the situation and D'Juana already knows she doesn't care much for Reo. So, she sighs loudly and says, "Naw, I just want to go home and lie down," in the most caring voice she can find within.

Lenese doesn't think twice about the ride home with Janard. It just feels so right and he seems to be right there whenever she needs him. This is the type of man she definitely needs in her life. This is how she always yearned for her and Antonio to be. Oh, they had their times, but it is never just comfortable and pleasurable like this. Janard is different. He has his shit together and knows what he wants out of life. He is a man's man and for Lenese that means everything. Every woman wants to feel secure over anything else.

Women want to know that their relationship, finances, and love are secure. The sad part is he is already married and very much taken. He actually wants his marriage to work, unlike most guys that come to Lenese for counseling. *How could I even consider having a real and true relationship with this man...the man of my dreams? I am always the first one to say, if he cheats on his wife, he will cheat on the other woman. But then again, he didn't cheat on his wife. His wife invited another woman into their bed and was very much involved.*

Lenese has a million and one things going through her mind right now. She picks up her cell phone to call and check on D'Juana and sees she has missed three calls from Antonio and a voice mail. *What the hell? He never leaves messages. Something must be wrong.* Lenese starts to listen to the voicemail and realizes that it just might add to the list of issues going on tonight.

Plus she doesn't want to disrespect Janard because she is sure whatever she hears, she will react. Just as she looks up at Janard and tries to take all this in and relax, she notices he is already looking at her with concern.

"Are you ok," he asks in a quiet but manly voice for the second time tonight. "Do you need anything? I have a pillow in the back and these seats do recline," he mentions very subtly while reaching as if he is going to grab the pillow for her whether she wants it or not.

Awww, he wants her to be comfortable. Her heart melts. Lenese doesn't need a pillow but because he wants to take care of her, she is going to take advantage of the situation. It's not too often she is pampered by a man she actually gives a fuck about. Hell, the thought crosses her mind that he can possibly be her man one day and she gets moist.

She wants to just reach over and suck the life out of his dick while he is driving, but he won't allow it. He is very different and that turns her on even more. Maybe it is just the fact that she can't have him that makes her want him even more. All she knows for sure is that he is the total package: puts it down in the bedroom, a provider, is loyal, and wants a family.

The little things like him being a communicator, caring, sensitive, etc., are all just icing on the cake. She wants to know how he feels without appearing to be desperate. She wants to look into his eyes and admit all the feelings that are inside of her, but she can't face rejection. She wants to see if the threesome changed any of the feelings he had for Enga while listening to and watching her with another woman. She just doesn't know how to break the ice.

Lenese feels Janard's tender hand on her shoulder gently lifting it up to slide the pillow behind her neck.

"Ohhhh, that's nice" she moans licking her lips seductively. That turns him on because before she can sit back on the pillow, he leans in closer kissing her with his arm still behind her neck. She wants to stop him and ask what all this means, but she thinks, *This shit feels so damn good that he doesn't have to leave the parking lot for all she cared.*

The kiss must be lasting at least five minutes and it is so intense and passionate. He stops kissing her only long enough to stare into her eyes or rub her face. He is kissing the shit out of her and if she doesn't know any better, it feels like she is busting a nut.

When he finally finishes pleasing her emotions, soul, and mouth, he sits back and takes a huge breath like he is about to pass out. What happens next is what changes Lenese's natural born life.

He looks her dead in the eyes, inhales, and says, "I want you more than life right now and forever. You are the star I've been wishing on all my life and I don't want to waste another moment wishing. I know we started off wrong, but if you let me, I will show you that I am your Mr. Right," he exhales.

Before Lenese can even ask the question that she's wanted to ask all night, he comes out and says, "I asked Enga for a divorce. We are at two different stages in our lives and I didn't realize that I was fighting a losing battle until we had the threesome."

As she lay there feeling like time just stopped and she and Janard are the only ones moving, her mouth drops open and she doesn't know whether to smile or pretend the news is shocking.

Oooohh, his confidence makes me squirm down below and I just want to jump on top of him and ride him like I've never rode anyone before. Damn, this man is so sexy to me. All this time they have been on the same page and she may finally get the man and the life she wants.

She smiles a smile of innocence and whispers, "I think I love you!"

You can have bought him for a nickel to hear those words come from Lenese's lips. Now he is eager to move forward and for the first time in his life, he feels love within his soul.

"Do you believe in love at first sight?" she asks still smiling and staring into his eyes.

"Well, I believe in God and I've never seen Him. I guess what I'm trying to say is, I believe that anything in life is possible and I can tell you that now, I also believe in miracles," Janard assures her.

A tear drops from Lenese's eyes and the emotions between them both run wild. She places her hand around the back of his neck to pull him closer to her lips so she can suck his face in. He loses sight of where they are and falls right into her charm.

They are kissing like newly- weds In a Big Red long lasting commercial and don't seem to care about their surroundings at the time. Lenese can actually feel the love spill from his heart through his lips and she intends on getting every last little bit of it because it is now, her time.

This was all she ever wanted and she's not going to allow anyone or anything to come between this "Enchanted Evening." At that very moment her song came on the radio and she isn't sure that she'd even heard the radio playing before. It is very low, but she can hear it and as Janet Jackson is singing "Any Time, Any Place" Lenese feels this is all meant to be and she will have to follow her heart for the first time in her life.

Janard is doing a wonderful job with his lips and tongue, but once the song comes on, Lenese can't keep still while her juices are flowing and she is grinding to the air as if she needs a warm body on top of her to complete the mission. She pulls him more firmly as if she wants him to come from behind the steering wheel and give her the business.

She realizes that although his C300 Mercedes Benz is very roomy and comfortable, she won't be able to do all the things she wants to do to him in the front seat of the car. So, she does what she can pushing him back to unzip his zipper, and pulls out his masterpiece to lick it like a pop cycle that is steadily melting….making sure not to waste any.

Chapter 22

Not Going Out Without A Fight

As Enga sits in her Jaguar with a look of disgust on her face, hurt in her eyes, and pain in her heart, she doesn't know what to say or do. She keeps telling herself that she should have never followed Janard to Kelly's that night, but she can't help but feel as though she is losing her mind on top of everything else.

She loves this man, but she didn't realize how much until she watched him walk out the door to begin a life without her. Yeah, she has been very selfish in their relationship and thought that everything was about her and her wants; well at first. Now, she knows that Janard is a good man and good men are very hard to find. All Janard wants to do is love her, keep her, protect her, and live the rest of his life with her just as he'd promise during their wedding vows.

Why am I so stupid? Why have I pushed him away? What is wrong with me? All of these thoughts cloud her mind as she sits there watching and waiting to see if the lovely couple will walk out of the bar together. Things just haven't been the same since she cheated on him with Desiree and she isn't even sure if she cared back then. *How could I screw something so good up the way I did?*

For the last 5 years, their entire marriage has been based on a lie. Enga is beautiful, smart, and outgoing. She can have any man she wants, but apparently she is willing to settle for the one who can take care of her financially. *How else can I expect this story to end? I must be dumb or just damn delusional to think a man as strong, caring, and secure as Janard would never see through my lies.*

Why did she waste so many years of his life knowing from the beginning what he wanted? Enga is well aware of Karma and how it works because she'd experienced it firsthand some years ago. She had dreams and aspirations of being a mother, wife, and career woman she is cursed. Her own mother is French-Creole and she isn't from Sweden at all, but from Louisiana.

She hates where she grew up and always dreamt of how she will escape until her mom fell sick from Cancer. She never cared for Enga because she hated for her own heritage. She is ashamed to be Creole and didn't believe in all the roots and stuff growing up. In fact, she downright despised everything about it.

Hell, she never fitted in anyway. She looked white with the blonde hair and blue eyes. She is the only child because her mother was raped and almost died giving birth to her. All Enga knew was she didn't want any parts of that voodoo mess and wanted to be as far away from it and her family as she possibly could.

So, at age seventeen when she got a call about doing an externship in Sweden, she jumped at the opportunity and didn't give one damn that her mother was dying and needed her. Her mother never forgave her for that. Enga remembers, as if it were yesterday, the look of desperation in her mother's eyes when she got down on her hands and knees and begged her to stay and help her through her last days on earth.

She can still hear the cries and it sends chills down her spine. She is ready to live her own life now and no one is going to stop her. Enga's mother pleaded with her not to make the mistake of treating her one and only mother that way, but Enga turned her back on her and walked away. What she heard next changed her life in ways that she never thought were possible.

She heard her mother chanting in some French Creole language that Enga never took the time to learn, and then took a deep breath which neither of them knew would be her last. All Enga heard was a thump as she turned to see her mother stretched out on the floor. Enga's cousin, Lauren, witnessed the whole ordeal and ran over to her aid.

"Are you just going to stand there and let her die?" she demanded of Enga with tears in her eyes and her voice trembling uncontrollably.

"What do you want from me? You take care of her. I have my own life to live. Plus, you've always been the perfect "daughter" anyway…the daughter she's never had" Enga said sarcastically as she began to walk out.

"Karma is a bitch and then you die" Lauren yelled out behind her.

Enga never looked back nor went back to Louisiana after that day. She never knew what her mom chanted about until she went to a carnival with a college friend and decided to get her fortune told. She never believed in those types of things especially because she grew up around it, but she was mortified when the fortune teller quoted the same exact thing her mother said to her on her dying day:

"Vous ne saurez jamais ce que c'est que d'etre mere. Vous etes condamnes a ne jamais avoir d'enfants." The fortune teller looked her in the eyes and said in a very quiet but believable voice, "You will never know what it's like to be a mother. You are cursed to never have children."

Of course Enga doesn't believe any of that mess, or does she? *How did the lady repeat exactly what my mother chanted to me on her death bed? There is only one way to be sure.* So, Enga goes to see her gynecologist and she confirms that Enga is "barren" which means, she will never be able to bear children. Right then Enga made an oath to learn her heritage, the French language, and to never speak a word of this madness to anyone, not even her closest friend or future husband.

Although Enga hides behind this hard shell and pretends as though she doesn't want kids, the news grazes her like a bullet. All she can do is accept what life has to offer and convinces herself that she can and will still have a happy and fulfilling life; even without children in it. She is still young and who knows what the future holds so she prayed and left it all in the hands of the Man upstairs.

She has built an empire with Janard and refuses to lose him to some bitch just because she can bear his babies. Just then "Ring the Alarm" by Beyoncé comes on the radio and it is just the boost of confidence and guts she needs to approach this situation head on. Just then, she sees the two walk out the bar together, and her blood starts boiling.

It feels like the walls are closing in on her as she can't really catch her breath from anxiety. When she sees them get into his car; the car she helped pick out, she is furious with rage and envy. She doesn't give a fuck that she'd invited this woman into their bed for her own personal reasons and it backfired. No, none of that matters anymore or especially not now.

Enga has never in her life been the vindictive type, but tonight she isn't in the right frame of mind. She is about to lose everything she's worked for and although she knows *Karma is the 'one bitch' that has everyone's address*, she isn't about ignored again…no, not this time. Janard isn't going to just leave her and let her struggle when she has been his everything for five Goddamn years. *Who the hell did Miss Freak Nasty think she is fuckin' with? I will kill that bitch before I see them happy together.*

When the words came out of her mouth and tears flow through her eyes, she can't believe what she just said. But, on the other hand, that isn't a bad idea at all. Enga is very sexy and can probably seduce some dumb ass dude to take care of Dr. No Good in no time. She'd even thought about using Voodoo on her and making her ass grow facial hair or something, but that won't be satisfaction enough for her...not tonight.

"Wait a minute. Stop the mutha fuckin' press," Enga yells out over the music as she watches Lenese's head disappear from the passenger head rest while Janard's head falls back on his own. *What the fuck is she doing? I know she is not giving him head in the fucking parking lot right at this moment;* disrespected and furious to say the least.

She can't believe what is going on in front of her face. She wants to get out of the car, walk over there, and snatch this bitch out through the window. That won't be wise though because there are too many witnesses out there. She can play the temporary insanity card, but then she will lose her money, job, and everything else she doesn't really care to live for anymore.

What is she going to do? She needs results and fast.

What she needs is for this woman to go the hell away even if she has to find way to do it herself. Hell, the way she is feeling tight now, she can walk up to her and blow her fucking brains out and Beyoncé isn't helping screaming the words:

"Ring the alarm. I've been through this too long. But I'll be damned if I see another chick on

*your arm... She gon' take everything I own If I let you go. I can't let you go...*Damn, if I let you go."

The words are ringing over and over again with the sirens in the background making Enga's blood boil hotter and has her thinking and believing she can actually get away with killing this woman. Especially when she hears: *"I done put in a call, time to ring the alarm 'Cause you ain't ever seen a fire like the one Imma 'cause."*

All of a sudden, she can't breathe watching Lenese's head come back up and Janard kissing her in the mouth with such passion; passion that he'd never shown her. About 2 minutes later, he is pulling out of the parking lot and Enga makes sure she is right on his tale and doesn't give a fuck if he sees her or not.

She isn't going to lose them by playing cops and robbers, staying 2 to 3 cars behind. Enga doesn't know what she plans on doing, how she will do it, or even if it will benefit her in the long run. But, she can' see past her anger and it is obvious that she is going to do something she may regret for the rest of her miserable, non-child bearing life.

Chapter 23

Prince *Charming* Janard

Janard is flying on cloud eleven right now and doesn't want to come down. He's always dreamt of having a strong, beautiful, successful woman by his side instead of a spoiled, selfish little girl that he has to finish raising and molding like Enga. Oh, Enga is absolutely gorgeous and every man's dream trophy wife, just not Janard's. He is much deeper than the surface and he needs much more than a physical connection.

He is a man who knows exactly what he wants out of life and that it takes hard work and Faith from the Man above to achieve it. He doesn't want things handed to him on a silver platter. He wants to make a life for himself and his family that he can be proud of. Janard is very old fashioned when it comes to his morals. He doesn't believe that a woman should have to work when she is married and that the man should be the bread-winner.

He is more impressed with Lenese than he actually lets on. She makes a career of helping people and that alone makes her special. Lenese shows elegance and grace. He remembers how she displayed nothing but professionalism towards him and Enga in their session. He was more surprised than excited about the fact that she was willing to go through with Enga's freaky idea of helping out the marriage of two consenting adults.

The only problem was Janard isn't dumb or ignorant by any means. He knew that his young wife had other intentions with the desirable Dr. Stringfield. He was even sure that she just wanted to have sex with this beautiful woman sitting to the side of him, and probably just wanted him to watch.

She really did look shocked to see him so intertwined with the beautiful doctor. He saw the pain and hurt in her eyes and for a moment, he felt like she was getting what she truly deserved. It's called Karma. What goes around always comes back around and he was enjoying every moment of it. His character usually doesn't call for this type of submission, but he wants to know how it feels to be on the giving end and not the receiving end for once.

Usually, he would have never agreed to such a thing because he looked at sex between a man and his wife as being something sacred. Since, his wife had already destroyed any possibility of living happily ever after with him, why should he sit around moping and crying over spilled milk?

The timing is as good as any to move forward in his life and leave whatever mishaps in the past. It hurts like a razor to let go and start anew, but he is a mover and a shaker. Life and time waits for no man and he knows firsthand that you get out of life, what you put into it.

Janard is a very mysterious man and Enga thinks she knows the secret that lies within. One day she was snooping through his things when they first started dating, but as far as she knows, he never found out. Janard comes from money and not just regular money. Janard is to inherit the throne of Bridgetown, Barbados. His grandmother is Queen Liza the second and she only has one child; his mother Elizabeth.

Sad enough, she is killed in an airplane crash along with Janard's father (Prince Janard II) when he is only 5 years old. This is the main reason Janard became a pilot, because he swore he would never trust someone else with his life as his parents did. It was and is his destiny to reign when he turns thirty-three years old, which is one short year from now. Enga knows that Janard is to be married before he can take the throne which is why she clenched her nails into him and held on for dear life.

What Enga doesn't know is that Janard doesn't want to reign as King of Barbados; he wants to live in America. He already made an arrangement with his grandmother not to take the throne, but receive a trust fund in the amount of ten million dollars instead under certain conditions. There are three conditions that Janard has to meet to be able to receive his trust fund and they are as follows:

1. He is to reach age 33.

2. He is to be married.

3. He is to have a child.

So, maybe he wasn't totally honest with his young, beautiful wife about his reasons for having children, but it doesn't matter now. He is stuck in a rut and he isn't sure how to approach the situation.

Maybe dear, little Enga isn't the only one holding on to this marriage for all the wrong reasons. It is just sad that he has wasted additional time staying with her when he could have been looking for his "future baby mama" and wife. It makes him feel sick to his stomach thinking about the consequences of leaving Enga so close to his deadline.

However, this thing, this love that he's found with Lenese is different and he wants to be more than honest with her. He wants to sit her down and tell her who he really is, but now he is scared. She just told him that she loves him, but she doesn't really love him, she loves the person she thinks she knows. *How did this happen? How did I continue on with these webs of lies to this wonderful woman whom I want to spend an eternity?* He isn't sure when or where, but he knows that he will definitely tell her soon and v very soon.

His grandmother made it very clear that if one of the three conditions isn't met, he will not be able to receive the trust fund and he will have to come back to Barbados to be throned or he will be disowned, knowing family means everything to her grandson. His stomach is churning like old butter and he doesn't want to think about all of this...not right now, not at that moment.

The real question is if he is willing to give all of that up for true love? This woman makes him feel amazing inside and out and he doesn't want to live another day without her. *Damn. Am I pussy- whipped or what?* He laughs out loud because he knows that isn't the case at all, forgetting he is in the car with this goddess.

Lenese turns to him with the most beautiful smile on her face and asks, "What are you laughing at?"

Caught off guard he quickly smiles back and says, "I am just thinking how lucky I am to be in your presence."

Whew, that was close, but I'm such a smooth operator, or at least he thinks for a brief moment, being very genuine at the same time. He's heard that he is just like his father, but never had a chance to really know. Janard does want a family, but because he was brought up fatherless, he isn't sure if he knows how to be a good dad and the thought alone haunted him every chance it got.

Being brought up by his grandmother, installed values like knowing how to love, honor, and respect women. Those are the characteristics that he is proud to have and make it easy for him to charm the pants off of any woman. But, he doesn't want to be known as being a womanizer at all. He wants to love only one and be truly loved by only one, which he feels would be easy to get from Lenese. That is IF she doesn't judge him off his own selfish intentions for holding on to his marriage as long as he did. He isn't sure if that will at all change her feelings for him as his woman and his counselor.

Janard takes a deep breath and begins to spill everything that is running through his mind and is trusting that love truly conquers all, when they see all the police cars, policeman directing traffic, fire trucks, and people standing outside of what looks like a tragic accident between an SUV and another car that he can't make out.

"OMG!" Lenese says, rising up from the supple leather that is hugging her entire body. "I wonder what happened and if the person driving the car burnt to a crisp is ok.

I can't even imagine what I would do if something like that happened to someone I love," leaning back to her comfort zone.

"I know what you mean,"

Janard exhales, shaking his head the entire time. It looks like they already transported the passengers to the hospital because there aren't any ambulances around.

He isn't sure if he'd been saved by the bell or just lost the confidence he had all together after that ordeal, but he knows deep down inside that this beautiful woman deserves to know the truth, the whole truth, and nothing but the truth. So, once again, he takes a deep breath to tell her his secret when he looks in his rearview mirror and sees a familiar car following them. Is that Enga?

What in the hell is she doing following him? Has this woman gone crazy or what? She never gave a damn about him or what he was doing before, so why now and how long has she been following him?

He quickly tries to replay his footsteps of the entire day after he left the house that morning and can't remember doing anything or really going anywhere except to the hotel. He wonders if she knows what hotel he is staying at and if she'd followed him there or did she call around?

All of that doesn't matter right now because he has just about had it with her shenanigans. He is going to confront her once and for all, but he clearly can't do it at Lenese's home. What is he going to do? He can't lead Enga to her home. He doesn't want to put her into harm's way even though he knows Enga won't bust a grape in a fruit fight. He has to make a detour to lose her, but how can he without Lenese wondering what is going on.

Damn, how the hell can I tell her that my wife is following us? They come to a four way intersection at Peachtree St. which is like the "Main St." of Atlanta, and he turns to Lenese and asks, "Which way beautiful?"

Smiling all over herself, she says, "Make a right and my house is the fifth one on the right!"

What the fuck? How the hell did she live so close and what am I going to do now? Janard can't seem to catch a break as he realizes he's going to have to man up and take charge of the situation.

It is clear that he can't duck Enga and it seems as if things are about to hit the damn fan. His palms get sweaty and he is feeling very uncomfortable, sitting up closer to the steering wheel. All he can do is try to remain cool and calm and pray that Enga doesn't get out of the car when he and Lenese does.

Chapter 24

Nothing But The Truth

There comes a time in your life when you realize what's good for you and what's not. The only thing is that sometimes it may be too late. And right now, Janard is thinking that his one shot of being happy is about to be ruined with drama from his lovely young wife. Things and people come and go in your life and you have to be prepared to take the good with the bad.

The shit is about to hit the fan and all he can do is try to avoid as much of it as humanly possible. He now knows that Enga isn't going out without a fight, but for the love of him, he can't figure out why. All of that doesn't matter now because she is about to show her perfect little ass and nothing but God can stop her.

As much as Janard wants to take his beautiful companion inside and make long, passionate, intense love to her, he can't. He has to make this sweet and simple by wrapping this drop off up as soon as possible or at least before Enga's crazy ass gets out of the car. So, he swings into the driveway of Lenese's home and gets out going around to open her door. Her big beautiful eyes follow his every movement with life and hopes of being taken in.

They are so gorgeous and captivating that he almost stumbles trying to hold himself together as his manhood is aching with pain and sheer lust. It feels like his dick is going to jump out of his pants as he pictures himself between Lenese's warm, meaty thighs. Focus Janard! He then takes Lenese by the hand to help her out of his car, kissing the back of her hand as if greeting his princess.

As she gets out of the car, she grabs him from behind and hugs his waist like teenagers in love will do. She is smiling and just happy to be in his presence and the feelings are well reciprocated, but not shown. Janard doesn't want to turn her off by rushing her up the stairs of her porch, but then again he does.

Knowing he can't make love to her is killing him and he wonders if she might call someone else over to finish the job he started. He wants to just put his hands between her long, amazing legs and feel all the moisture that better be just for him. Although she's told him that she is in love with him, they haven't made anything official and unfortunately he can't seal the deal tonight.

Lenese looks into her purse for the car keys, once they reach the top step. Janard sees Enga turn the corner and begins to panic. He is feeling antsy and can't pull it together.

"What's wrong," Lenese asks because she can see the look of fear in his eyes.

"Oh, nothing baby. I just really need to use your restroom," he replies.

What the fuck was I thinking? I'm not supposed to go in. I'm supposed to stay outside and get rid of Enga's crazy ass. Now I have to wonder if she will have enough gumption to knock on this woman's door and that is worse than talking to her outside.

"Ok lover, we're in," Lenese says as she opens the door and slowly walks into her humble abode. "The bathroom is down the hall to the right my love slave," she whispers and nibbles on his ear in the most seductive voice she has inside of her.

Lenese is ready for this moment and nothing will or can ruin it. Well at least that's what she thought as her cell phone starts ringing off the hook again. This time it isn't Antonio though, it is his sister, Lexy. What in the world does Lexy want? Lenese wonders.

I bet he got her to call because I am not answering his calls. How childish and desperate can his ass be? Then again, Lexy isn't the type to get into their business like that and maybe she should call her back or at least listen to the voicemail message she just left to make sure everything is ok.

What she heard on that voicemail changed her life forever in a way that only God, Himself knew. As Janard is coming out of the bathroom, all he sees is this beautiful creature on her knees in the middle of the hallway floor, crying out loud, and shaking like a leaf on a tree. The phone is lying on the floor in front of her and she is covering her face with her hands while rocking back and forth.

"What in the world is wrong with you gorgeous?" Janard asks in a demanding kind of voice.

"What happened so fast?" All kinds of thoughts went through his head as to what could have happened.

"Baby, please talk to me," he begs lifting her off the floor and embracing her tight up against his body.

"I need to go. I just need to get out of here. she cries out in a desperate but forceful voice.

She pulls away from Janard reluctantly, grabs her purse, and is halfway out the door before he can even take a breath to process everything that is happening.

Lenese feels numb and doesn't have time to explain the message or anything else for that matter. She just needs to get to the hospital as soon as possible and be there for the love of her life as he would be there for her. Janard doesn't matter right now. In fact, Lenese feels like all of this is her fault. *Why didn't I just answer the damn phone when he was trying to call me?*

Life changes when you least expect it and right now, Lenese is experiencing it firsthand. She literally doesn't know what to do with herself. She grabs the door knob opening her front door only to find the last person in the world that she expected to be on her damn door step...Enga!

"What the fuck are you doing here?" Lenese scolds her. Her eyes are blood shot red and still full of tears and she doesn't have the time or the patience to deal with this shit right now. "Get the fuck off my property!" yelling at Enga with an estranged look in her eyes.

"You think you can just come into my life and take away everything I have? You think that your perfect little life can never be altered, huh?" Enga demands.

Janard heard Enga at the door and immediately runs out in front of Lenese grabbing Enga and pushing her back down the porch stairs to solid ground. Enga is resisting and still yelling out slurs to Lenese as Janard pushes her back towards her car.

"You think you got it all figured out don't you? You're no better than me you know? Fucking all your male, MARRIED clients to make their relationships better! How the fuck does that work? You are the worse type of whore!"

Janard can't believe his ears. *Is Enga lying to make me feel some type of way about Lenese or is all this true? Why would she say such things? Then again, what even gives Enga the right to be there or to ask any damn questions?*

"Enga, get the fuck out of here." he says in a voice deeper than James Earl Jones's.

"I will kill that bitch before I let her take you away from me!" Enga screams to the top of her lungs.

Lenese acted as if she did not hear a word Enga said and that is because she truly does not. Her ears are clouded and everything is coming out in mumbles.

All she remembers seeing is Janard pushing Enga out of her way and she doesn't really give a fuck about the rest. All Lenese can think about is getting to the hospital to be there for Antonio while silently praying that he is okay and going to live. The message Lexy left was erratic and unclear and the mindset Lenese is in right now doesn't call for any conversation. She wants to get there as soon as possible to find out for herself.

Right at that moment, she has a "vision" so to speak. She is reliving a moment or at least that's how it feels. *Oh my dear God. This is the damn nightmare coming true.* She can finally see that the nightmares she's been having that were so unclear to her, is of Antonio getting into an accident with some sort of SUV with his car bursting into flames, which is the point when she will always wake up.

Dammit! I wonder if that accident we passed was him. She becomes extremely jittery waiting for the garage door to go up so she can get in the fuckin her car and leave the madness. The next thing Lenese knows, she hears a gunshot that sounds close like a rocket. She slowly turns to see Enga holding a gun. The air leaves her body and all her blood rushes to her head; and she loses sight of life as she falls to the ground.

TO BE CONTINUED
IN VOLUME 2
OF:
"THE SEXCAPADES"